The Brontë Sisters

The Works of
The Brontë Sisters

with an Introduction by Kathryn White,
and Bibliography

Wordsworth Poetry Library

This edition published 1995 by Wordsworth Editions Ltd,
Cumberland House, Crib Street, Ware, Hertfordshire SG12 9ET.

Copyright © Wordsworth Editions Ltd 1995.

ISBN 1-85326-440-7

Typeset in the UK by Antony Gray.
Printed and bound in Denmark by Nørhaven.

The paper in this book is produced from pure wood
pulp, without the use of chlorine or any other substance
harmful to the environment. The energy used in its
production consists almost entirely of hydroelectricity
and heat generated from waste materials, thereby
conserving fossil fuels and contributing little to the
greenhouse effect.

INTRODUCTION

In her 'Biographical Notice of Ellis and Acton Bell', published in the 1850 edition of *Wuthering Heights* and *Agnes Grey*, Charlotte Brontë recalled the decision to adopt pseudonyms: 'Averse to personal publicity, we veiled our own names under those of Currer, Ellis, and Acton Bell; the ambiguous choice being dictated by a sort of conscientious scruple at assuming Christian names positively masculine, while we did not like to declare ourselves women, because – without at that time suspecting that our mode of writing and thinking was not what is called 'feminine' – we had a vague impression that authoresses are liable to be looked on with prejudice . . . ' The pseudonyms used for the Brontë sisters' collection of poetry, published as *Poems* by Currer, Ellis and Acton Bell in 1846, gave rise to inevitable speculation about the authors' identities, a trend which gathered momentum with the publication of their novels the following year.

Charlotte recounted in the Biographical Notice how the poems came to be published: 'One day, in the autumn of 1845, I accidentally lighted on a MS volume of verse in my sister Emily's handwriting . . . something more than surprise seized me – a deep conviction that these were not common effusions, nor at all like the poetry women generally write. I thought them condensed and terse, vigorous and genuine. To my ear, they also had a peculiar music – wild, melancholy, and elevating.' Emily was incensed at this invasion of her privacy as, in later years, the three sisters' writing had become less of a shared activity and it took Charlotte some time to persuade Emily that her poems should be published. As Ellis Bell, Emily retained her anonymity to her death, but Charlotte enjoyed literary fame after the deaths of her sisters. Charlotte is acknowledged as the lesser poet of the Brontë family. Her talents lay in prose and her poetry is stilted by an adherence to regular versification, while Anne's poetry has a truth and simplicity which elevate it above that of her eldest sister, and Emily is generally recognised as a poet of original power and genius.

In January 1846, Charlotte secured the services of Aylott & Jones of London, who were to publish the poems 'on the Authors' account'. When this small volume by unknown authors first appeared, in a period when the poetry market was in the doldrums, it excited little interest. The edition sold just two copies and received few reviews; these, although praising the quality of the poems, were more fascinated by the mystery of authorship. *The Critic* of 4 July 1846 commented, ' . . . it is long since we have enjoyed a volume of such genuine poetry as this', while *The Athenaeum* of the same date praised Ellis's '. . . fine quaint spirit . . . an evident power of wing that may reach heights not here attempted'.

The poems can be appreciated in isolation, but a knowledge of the Brontës' biographical background aids an understanding of their work and it is essential to see the Brontës as a family unit. The family produced five published poets: Charlotte, Emily, Anne, their father Patrick and brother Branwell. Branwell Brontë, often portrayed as a drunken wastrel, actually saw his poems in print in the local newspapers as early as 1841, five years before his sisters were published. His work, especially his translations of the first book of the *Odes of Quintus Horatius Flaccus*, unpublished during his lifetime, is well regarded. John Drinkwater, in his 1923 edition of Branwell's translation, commented on Branwell's passages of 'clear lyrical beauty' and his 'spiritual understanding' of classical models. Hartley Coleridge whom Branwell visited in the Lake District in 1840 was particularly impressed by Branwell's work. Unfortunately finances and lack of self–discipline prevented Branwell from achieving his potential. Presumably Branwell, once the driving force of their childhood creativity, was excluded from his sisters' publication project because he had been dismissed from his post as tutor to the Robinson family in July 1845 after a romantic entanglement with his employer's wife. From then onwards he was in a state of emotional turmoil with which Charlotte especially found it hard to sympathise. The Reverend Patrick Brontë produced several collections of didactic poetry, such as *Cottage Poems* (1811) and *The Rural Minstrel* (1813), phrased in what he described as 'simple' language, and designed for the enjoyment and religious instruction of the working classes. His works have been criticised somewhat unfairly as pedestrian in comparison with those of his children, but it has to be remembered that he was addressing an entirely different audience.

Thus the young Brontës would have been familiar with the family name on book spines around the house. In their parsonage home at Haworth, the children read reviews of poetry and books in periodicals such as *Blackwood's Edinburgh Magazine* and were instructed in the Classics by their Cambridge-educated father. Unusually for young women in the early nineteenth century, the Brontës were not restricted in their reading and were allowed access to the complete works of Byron and Shakespeare. In a letter of 4 July 1834, the eighteen-year-old Charlotte advised her more conventional friend Ellen Nussey on reading material, thus supplying us with evidence of the Brontës' own formative reading: 'If you like poetry let it be first rate, Milton, Shakespeare, Thomson, Goldsmith, Pope (if you will, though I don't admire him), Scott, Byron, Campbell, Wordsworth and Southey.'

It is difficult to pinpoint the precise influences which shaped the Brontës' poetic vision but some understanding of their early writings is helpful to an appreciation of the poems. From an early age the Brontës had composed prose and poetry and Charlotte recalled that they had ' . . . very early cherished the dream of one day becoming authors'. The Brontës' literary apprenticeship began with the creation of a web of tales and adventures woven around their toy soldiers, recorded in hand-made little books, some less than two inches high, in tiny handwriting to resemble print. As the stories grew more complex they retained the minuscule hand for their private writings, and the prose and poetry of their imaginary lands: Charlotte and Branwell's Angria and Emily and Anne's Gondal, which featured battles, romance, artists, poets, debauchery, humour and tragedy. The Brontës themselves edited their poems for publication in 1846 to remove any traces of their private world. Some of the poems have their basis in Angria and Gondal, while others reflect personal themes.

In 1836, Charlotte, then an unhappy teacher at Roe Head School, unable to resolve the inner conflict between the 'infernal world' of the imagination and the duties of everyday life, wrote to the Poet Laureate, Southey, who responded to the eager young woman with the now famous words, 'Literature cannot be the business of a woman's life, and it ought not to be.' He added that she should 'write poetry for its own sake; not in a spirit of emulation, and not with a view to celebrity; the less you aim at that the more likely you will be to deserve and finally to obtain it'.

Of the nineteen poems by Charlotte in the 1846 edition, thirteen were written in 1837 when she was just twenty-one years old, and the rest at irregular intervals. 'The Teacher's Monologue', written at Roe Head School in 1837, is an expression of frustration and homesickness; a fear of spending life in the 'wretched bondage' with which Charlotte was familiar as both teacher and governess. Writing was one of the few career options open to educated women in the mid-nineteenth century. 'The Teacher's Monologue' is autobiographical, while the remainder of Charlotte's poems in the 1846 edition seem to originate in Angrian themes and settings. During the periods when she was earning a living her poetic output dried up. There are few extant poems after 1840 and no poetry dating from her time as a student in Brussels, when she conceived a passionate and unrequited admiration for her tutor, Constantin Heger. Charlotte's poems are of interest today chiefly as the formative work of the author of *Jane Eyre*.

Charlotte recognised that her poetic ability was limited, unlike that of her sister Emily whose poetry has been compared to that of William Blake and Emily Dickinson. It is difficult to know how far Emily's poems related to her own feelings and the extent to which they refer to Gondal characters. No Gondal prose by Emily or Anne survives, but Emily's poems included in the 1846 edition were transcribed from two extant manuscript notebooks. The Gondal poems explore lyrically emotional themes of passionate love and revenge, as does Emily's only novel, *Wuthering Heights*. 'The Old Stoic', with its desire for a 'chainless soul', may be Gondal-based or personal for, as Charlotte stated in 1850, 'Liberty was the breath of Emily's nostrils; without it, she perished.' Liberty is also invoked in 'To Imagination', written in September 1844, in which Emily reconciles the difference between reality and imagination; something which Charlotte struggled to achieve. However, in 'The Philosopher' death is seen as an end rather than expressive of liberty. 'Remembrance' is a Gondal poem of 3 March 1845, a lyrical lament for a lost love, perhaps prefiguring Heathcliff's love for Cathy which survives for years after her death. Themes of exile and physical and spiritual imprisonment echo the anguish of Heathcliff the outcast. 'The Prisoner', which features a powerful, mystical experience, was revised and shortened from a Gondal poem, 'Julian M. to A. G. Rochelle', and the last stanza was added for the 1846 publication. Emily's poetry points out the apparent irrelevance of life's trials and expresses a belief in a transcendent power. This belief is expressed most strongly in 'No Coward Soul is Mine', first published in 1850, and included in the Gondal poems notebooks, but may represent Emily's personal vision of a God of Nature rather than the conventional Christian God.

In contrast to Emily's unique vision of God, A. C. Benson, writing in 1913, considered that Anne's poetry had a 'cramping kind of orthodox piety', but he did not take into account how Charlotte edited Anne's work after her death and suppressed the reprinting of *The Tenant of Wildfell Hall*, the powerful content of which she considered 'an entire mistake'. 'Last Lines', not included in this edition, was written in January 1849 when Anne became aware that she was likely to die from tuberculosis. The poem was edited severely by Charlotte in 1850 to make Anne appear more accepting of death, while the manuscript reveals Anne's fear and confusion. 'A Reminiscence', written in April 1844, is usually seen as a celebration of the life of her father's curate, William Weightman, who died in 1842. 'Music on Christmas Morning' expresses a quiet Christianity and certainty that God would redeem all sinners. 'Home' contrasts the environment of formal garden borders which Anne experienced in her five years' employment as a governess at Thorp Green with the weeds usurping the ground in the garden at home at Haworth, echoing the 'garden-walk with weeds o'er-grown' in Emily's 'A Little While, a Little While', written in December 1838 when she was a desperately homesick teacher at Law Hill. 'If This be All' is an unusually pessimistic poem written just before Branwell was dismissed from Thorp Green and reflecting Anne's despair at his conduct. Anne's poetry, like her novels, has been underrated for many years.

The publisher of Charlotte's novels, Smith, Elder & Co., bought the unsold copies of *Poems* and re-issued them in 1848 in the wake of the success of *Jane Eyre*. This edition follows the text of the 1846 first edition, and the poems, showing how the Brontës wished to present their work to the public, represent only a small proportion of their poetic output. Complete editions of the Brontë poems have been edited by Edward Chitham, C. W. Hatfield, Janet Gezari and Victor Neufeldt.

CHARLOTTE BRONTË (1816–55) was born on 21 April 1816 at Thornton, near Bradford in Yorkshire. She was the third child of the Reverend Patrick Brontë (1777–1861) and his Cornish wife Maria Branwell (1783–1821). Patrick came from a poor background in Ireland to St John's College, Cambridge to train as a clergyman. He held several posts before becoming perpetual curate of Haworth, near Keighley in Yorkshire in 1820, where he remained until his death at the age of eighty-four in 1861. Charlotte's mother died on 15 September 1821, after which the Brontë children were cared for by their aunt, Elizabeth Branwell.

Charlotte was the older sister of Emily, Anne, and her brother, Branwell (1817–48), with whom she collaborated in their early writings about the fictional land of Angria. Sadly, Branwell failed to realise his early promise as an artist and writer.

The Brontës had no private income and, since the parsonage belonged to the Church rather than to their father, his children were educated with a view to earning their own livings, as it was assumed that Mr Brontë would die before his children. Thus Charlotte, like Emily, attended the Clergy Daughters' School at Cowan Bridge, Kirby Lonsdale in Yorkshire from 1824–5. The two eldest Brontë children, Maria and Elizabeth, died aged eleven and ten as a result of the poor conditions at the school and Charlotte used the memory of this early loss in her portrayal of Lowood

School in *Jane Eyre*. The four remaining Brontë children were educated at home for the next few years until Charlotte attended Roe Head School at Mirfield, near Dewsbury from 1831–2. It was here that she met her lifelong friends Ellen Nussey and Mary Taylor. Charlotte then taught Emily and Anne at home before returning to Roe Head as a teacher between 1835 and 1838, after which she spent some time working as a governess in two private households. Charlotte hated being a dependant and in 1842 she proposed that the sisters should run a school from the parsonage. She and Emily travelled to Brussels that year to improve their languages, enrolling as pupils at the Pensionnat Heger. It was here that Charlotte conceived a deep but unrequited admiration for her married tutor, Constantin Heger. Her experiences in Brussels formed the basis of her novels *Villette* and *The Professor*. Charlotte returned to Haworth in 1844.

In 1846, *Poems* by Currer, Ellis and Acton Bell was published and soon afterwards Charlotte's first novel, *The Professor*, was offered unsuccessfully to various publishers. The novel was eventually published posthumously in 1857. Meanwhile from August 1846 until its completion a year later Charlotte worked on *Jane Eyre*, which was published in October 1847 by Smith Elder & Co. in the standard three-volume format under the pseudonym Currer Bell. The novel met with instant success. Charlotte wrote two further novels, *Shirley* (1849) and *Villette* (1853), which were also published under her pseudonym. After the deaths of Emily and Anne, Charlotte enjoyed literary fame and made several visits to London, where she stayed with the family of her publisher, George Smith. She met Harriet Martineau, Elizabeth Gaskell and W. M. Thackeray, whose work she admired greatly.

Charlotte Brontë had refused marriage proposals in the past but eventually accepted her father's curate, the Revd Arthur Bell Nicholls. They were married on 29 June 1854 but, after a few happy months, Charlotte Brontë died aged thirty-eight at Haworth on 31 March 1855, of an illness most probably associated with pregnancy. She is buried in the family vault beneath Haworth church, with the rest of her family except Anne, who is buried in Scarborough on the Yorkshire coast. Charlotte's unfinished novel, *Emma,* was published in 1860 with an introduction by Thackeray. After the death of Patrick Brontë in 1861, Charlotte's husband returned to Ireland, later marrying his cousin, Mary Bell. Arthur Bell Nicholls, the last direct link to the Brontës of Haworth, died in 1906 at the age of eighty-eight.

EMILY BRONTË (1818–48) was born on 30 July 1818 at Thornton. She was the fifth child of Patrick and Maria Brontë, the younger sister of

Charlotte and older sister of Anne, to whom she was very close. At the age of six, Emily attended the Clergy Daughters' School at Cowan Bridge for a brief period. In July 1835 she accompanied Charlotte to Roe Head School as a free pupil. Feeling homesick, she returned to Haworth after just a few months and her place was taken by Anne. In September 1838 Emily became a teacher at Law Hill School near Halifax but similarly remained there only a few months. In 1842 she accompanied Charlotte to Brussels but, unlike Charlotte, the experience seems to have had little effect on her writing. Of all the Brontës, Emily was the most influenced by the wild moorland scenery around her home at Haworth. Emily died of consumption, or tuberculosis as it is now known, at the age of thirty on 19 December 1848, the year following the publication of *Wutherings Heights*. Emily's poetry and prose are amongst the most highly regarded works in the English language. Only a handful of Emily's personal papers and manuscripts have survived and she remains an enigma to readers and biographers alike.

ANNE BRONTË (1820–49) was Emily's younger sister, with whom she invented the imaginary world of Gondal. Anne was the sixth and youngest child of Patrick and Maria Brontë, moving to Haworth the year following her birth. Her mother died before Anne was two years old. Too young to attend the Cowan Bridge school with her sisters, Anne was largely educated at home. She first went to school at the age of fifteen, replacing Emily as a free pupil at Roe Head, where Charlotte was now a teacher. Anne left the school in December 1837.

In April 1839 Anne took up the post of governess to the Ingham family at Blake Hall, Mirfield. In May 1840 she became governess to the Robinsons of Thorp Green, Little Ouseburn, near York, where she remained until June 1845. She was joined by her brother Branwell in January 1843 when he became tutor to the Robinsons' son. Shortly after Anne's departure, Branwell was dismissed from his post because he had become emotionally entangled with his employer's wife, Mrs Lydia Robinson, a trauma from which he never fully recovered.

Anne's first novel, *Agnes Grey*, was published along with Emily's *Wuthering Heights* in December 1847 and her second, *The Tenant of Wildfell Hall,* appeared in June 1848. Thomas Cautley Newby, Emily and Anne's publisher, had given the impression that Currer, Ellis and Acton Bell were a single author in order to capitalise on the success of *Jane Eyre*. In July 1848, Anne travelled to London with Charlotte to prove to Charlotte's publishers, Smith, Elder & Co., that the 'Bells' were at least two authors.

Anne's work has often been underrated and she is usually seen in the shadow of her sisters. Because little manuscript material survives, like Emily, we see Anne Brontë through her sister Charlotte's eyes. Charlotte thought that the choice of subject matter for *The Tenant of Wildfell Hall* was 'an entire mistake' and she suppressed further publication of this novel following Anne's death.

On 24 September 1848 Branwell died, and Emily died on 19 December. Anne was diagnosed as suffering from tuberculosis in January 1849 and she travelled to Scarborough in May in the hope of a sea cure. She died there on 28 May 1849, aged just twenty-nine, and is buried in St Mary's churchyard, overlooking the sea.

Anne's short life, together with those of her remarkable family, is firmly established as one of the literary legends of the British Isles. Their novels and poems are read and studied worldwide and their former home, now the Brontë Parsonage Museum, has been visited by over six million people since it opened in 1928.

Kathryn White
Brontë Parsonage Museum

FURTHER READING

Christine Alexander, *The Early Writings of Charlotte Brontë*, Oxford: Basil Blackwell, 1983

Juliet Barker, *The Brontës*, London: Weidenfeld & Nicolson, 1994

Juliet Barker (ed.), *The Brontës: Selected Poems*, London: Everyman, 1993

Charlotte Brontë, 'Biographical Notice of Ellis and Acton Bell' and 'Editor's Preface to the New Edition of *Wuthering Heights*', 1850. Reprinted in most modern editions of the novel

Edward Chitham (ed.), *The Poems of Anne Brontë*, London: Macmillan, 1979

Elizabeth Gaskell, *The Life of Charlotte Brontë*, first published 1857; Penguin Books 1975

Janet Gezari (ed.), *Emily Jane Brontë: The Complete Poems*, London: Penguin Books, 1992

Victor Neufeldt (ed.), *The Poems of Charlotte Brontë*, New York: Garland Publishing Inc., 1988

Margaret Smith (ed.), *The Letters of Charlotte Brontë*, Oxford University Press, 1995

CONTENTS

POEMS

BY

CURRER, ELLIS, AND ACTON

BELL.

———

LONDON:
AYLOTT AND JONES, 8, PATERNOSTER-ROW.
——
1846.

The title page of the first edition

Pilate's Wife's Dream

I've quenched my lamp, I struck it in that start
Which every limb convulsed, I heard it fall –
The crash blent with my sleep, I saw depart
Its light, even as I woke, on yonder wall;
Over against my bed, there shone a gleam
Strange, faint, and mingling also with my dream.

It sunk, and I am wrapt in utter gloom;
How far is night advanced, and when will day
Retinge the dusk and livid air with bloom,
And fill this void with warm, creative ray?
Would I could sleep again till, clear and red,
Morning shall on the mountain-tops be spread!

I'd call my women, but to break their sleep,
Because my own is broken, were unjust;
They've wrought all day, and well-earned slumbers steep
Their labours in forgetfulness, I trust;
Let me my feverish watch with patience bear,
Thankful that none with me its sufferings share.

Yet, Oh, for light! one ray would tranquillise
My nerves, my pulses, more than effort can;
I'll draw my curtain and consult the skies:
These trembling stars at dead of night look wan,
Wild, restless, strange, yet cannot be more drear
Than this my couch, shared by a nameless fear.

All black – one great cloud, drawn from east to west,
Conceals the heavens, but there are lights below;
Torches burn in Jerusalem, and cast
On yonder stony mount a lurid glow.
I see men stationed there, and gleaming spears;
A sound, too, from afar, invades my ears.

Dull, measured, strokes of axe and hammer ring
From street to street; not loud, but through the night
Distinctly heard – and some strange spectral thing
Is now upreared – and, fixed against the light
Of the pale lamps; defined upon that sky,
It stands up like a column, straight and high.

I see it all – I know the dusky sign –
A cross on Calvary, which Jews uprear
While Romans watch; and when the dawn shall shine
Pilate, to judge the victim will appear,
Pass sentence – yield him up to crucify;
And on that cross the spotless Christ must die.

Dreams, then, are true – for thus my vision ran;
Surely some oracle has been with me,
The gods have chosen me to reveal their plan,
To warn an unjust judge of destiny:
I, slumbering, heard and saw; awake I know,
Christ's coming death, and Pilate's life of woe.

I do not weep for Pilate – who could prove
Regret for him whose cold and crushing sway
No prayer can soften, no appeal can move;
Who tramples hearts as others trample clay,
Yet with a faltering, an uncertain tread,
That might stir up reprisal in the dead.

Forced to sit by his side and see his deeds;
Forced to behold that visage, hour by hour,
In whose gaunt lines, the abhorrent gazer reads
A triple lust of gold, and blood, and power;
A soul whom motives, fierce, yet abject, urge
Rome's servile slave, and Judah's tyrant scourge.

How can I love, or mourn, or pity him?
I, who so long my fettered hands have wrung;
I, who for grief have wept my eye-sight dim;
Because, while life for me was bright and young,
He robbed my youth – he quenched my life's fair ray –
He crushed my mind, and did my freedom slay.

And at this hour – although I be his wife –
He has no more of tenderness from me
Than any other wretch of guilty life;
Less, for I know his household privacy –
I see him as he is – without a screen;
And, by the gods, my soul abhors his mien!

Has he not sought my presence, dyed in blood –
Innocent, righteous blood, shed shamelessly?
And have I not his red salute withstood?
Aye, – when, as erst, he plunged all Galilee
In dark bereavement – in affliction sore,
Mingling their very offerings with their gore.

Then came he – in his eyes a serpent-smile,
Upon his lips some false, endearing word,
And, through the streets of Salem, clanged the while,
His slaughtering, hacking, sacrilegious sword –
And I, to see a man cause men such woe,
Trembled with ire – I did not fear to show.

And now, the envious Jewish priests have brought
Jesus – whom they in mockery call their king –
To have, by this grim power, their vengeance wrought;
By this mean reptile, innocence to sting.
Oh! could I but the purposed doom avert,
And shield the blameless head from cruel hurt!

Accessible is Pilate's heart to fear,
Omens will shake his soul, like autumn leaf;
Could he this night's appalling vision hear,
This just man's bonds were loosed, his life were safe,
Unless that bitter priesthood should prevail,
And make even terror to their malice quail.

Yet if I tell the dream – but let me pause.
What dream? Erewhile the characters were clear,
Graved on my brain – at once some unknown cause
Has dimmed and rased the thoughts, which now appear,
Like a vague remnant of some by-past scene; –
Not what will be, but what, long since, has been.

I suffered many things, I heard foretold
A dreadful doom for Pilate, – lingering woes,
In far, barbarian climes, where mountains cold
Built up a solitude of trackless snows,
There, he and grisly wolves prowled side by side,
There he lived famished – there methought he died;

But not of hunger, nor by malady;
I saw the snow around him, stained with gore;
I said I had no tears for such as he,
And, lo! my cheek is wet – mine eyes run o'er;
I weep for mortal suffering, mortal guilt,
I weep the impious deed the blood self-spilt.

More I recall not, yet the vision spread
Into a world remote, an age to come –
And still the illumined name of Jesus shed
A light, a clearness, through the unfolding gloom –
And still I saw that sign, which now I see,
That cross on yonder brow of Calvary.

What is this Hebrew Christ? To me unknown,
His lineage – doctrine – mission – yet how clear,
Is God-like goodness, in his actions shewn!
How straight and stainless is his life's career!
The ray of Deity that rests on him,
In my eyes makes Olympian glory dim.

The world advances, Greek, or Roman rite
Suffices not the inquiring mind to stay;
The searching soul demands a purer light
To guide it on its upward, onward way;
Ashamed of sculptured gods – Religion turns
To where the unseen Jehovah's altar burns.

Our faith is rotten – all our rites defiled,
Our temples sullied, and methinks, this man,
With his new ordinance, so wise and mild,
Is come, even as he says, the chaff to fan
And sever from the wheat; but will his faith
Survive the terrors of tomorrow's death?

* * *

I feel a firmer trust – a higher hope
Rise in my soul – it dawns with dawning day;
Lo! on the Temple's roof – on Moriah's slope
Appears at length that clear, and crimson ray,
Which I so wished for when shut in by night;
Oh, opening skies, I hail, I bless your light!

Part, clouds and shadows! glorious Sun appear!
Part, mental gloom! Come insight from on high!
Dusk dawn in heaven still strives with daylight clear,
The longing soul, doth still uncertain sigh.
Oh! to behold the truth – that sun divine,
How doth my bosom pant, my spirit pine!

This day, time travails with a mighty birth,
This day, Truth stoops from heaven and visits earth,
Ere night descends, I shall more surely know
What guide to follow, in what path to go;
I wait in hope – I wait in solemn fear,
The oracle of God – the sole – true God – to hear.

CURRER

Faith and Despondency

'The winter wind is loud and wild,
Come close to me, my darling child;
Forsake thy books, and mateless play;
And, while the night is gathering grey,
We'll talk its pensive hours away; –

   'Iernë, round our sheltered hall
November's gusts unheeded call;
Not one faint breath can enter here
Enough to wave my daughter's hair,
And I am glad to watch the blaze
Glance from her eyes, with mimic rays;
To feel her cheek, so softly pressed,
In happy quiet on my breast.

   'But, yet, even this tranquillity
Brings bitter, restless thoughts to me;
And, in the red fire's cheerful glow,
I think of deep glens, blocked with snow;
I dream of moor, and misty hill,
Where evening closes dark and chill;
For, lone, among the mountains cold,
Lie those that I have loved of old.
And my heart aches, in hopeless pain
Exhausted with repinings vain,
That I shall greet them ne'er again!'

   'Father, in early infancy,
When you were far beyond the sea,
Such thoughts were tyrants over me!
I often sat, for hours together,
Through the long nights of angry weather,
Raised on my pillow, to descry
The dim moon struggling in the sky;
Or, with strained ear, to catch the shock,
Of rock with wave, and wave with rock;

So would I fearful vigil keep,
And, all for listening, never sleep.
But this world's life has much to dread,
Not so, my Father, with the dead.

   'Oh! not for them, should we despair,
The grave is drear, but they are not there;
Their dust is mingled with the sod,
Their happy souls are gone to God!
You told me this, and yet you sigh,
And murmur that your friends must die.
Ah! my dear father, tell me why?
For, if your former words were true,
How useless would such sorrow be;
As wise, to mourn the seed which grew
Unnoticed on its parent tree,
Because it fell in fertile earth,
And sprang up to a glorious birth –
Struck deep its root, and lifted high
Its green boughs, in the breezy sky.

   'But, I'll not fear, I will not weep
For those whose bodies rest in sleep, –
I know there is a blessed shore,
   Opening its ports for me, and mine;
And, gazing Time's wide waters o'er,
   I weary for that land divine,
Where we were born, where you and I
Shall meet our Dearest, when we die;
From suffering and corruption free,
Restored into the Deity.'

   'Well hast thou spoken, sweet, trustful child!
   And wiser than thy sire;
And worldly tempests, raging wild,
   Shall strengthen thy desire –
Thy fervent hope, through storm and foam,
   Through wind and ocean's roar,
To reach, at last, the eternal home,
   The steadfast, changeless, shore!'

ELLIS

A Reminiscence

Yes, thou art gone! and never more
Thy sunny smile shall gladden me;
But I may pass the old church door,
And pace the floor that covers thee,

May stand upon the cold, damp stone,
And think that, frozen, lies below
The lightest heart that I have known,
The kindest I shall ever know.

Yet, though I cannot see thee more,
'Tis still a comfort to have seen;
And though thy transient life is o'er,
'Tis sweet to think that thou hast been;

To think a soul so near divine,
Within a form, so angel fair,
United to a heart like thine,
Has gladdened once our humble sphere.

ACTON

Mementos

Arranging long-locked drawers and shelves
Of cabinets, shut up for years,
What a strange task we've set ourselves!
How still the lonely room appears!
How strange this mass of ancient treasures,
Mementos of past pains and pleasures;
These volumes, clasped with costly stone,
With print all faded, gilding gone;
These fans of leaves, from Indian trees –
These crimson shells, from Indian seas –
These tiny portraits, set in rings –
Once, doubtless, deemed such precious things;
Keepsakes bestowed by Love on Faith,
And worn till the receiver's death,
Now stored with cameos, china, shells,
In this old closet's dusty cells.

I scarcely think, for ten long years,
A hand has touched these relics old;
And, coating each, slow-formed, appears,
The growth of green and antique mould.

All in this house is mossing over;
All is unused, and dim, and damp;
Nor light, nor warmth, the rooms discover –
Bereft for years of fire and lamp.

The sun, sometimes in summer, enters
The casements, with reviving ray;
But the long rains of many winters
Moulder the very walls away.

And outside all is ivy, clinging
To chimney, lattice, gable grey;
Scarcely one little red rose springing
Through the green moss can force its way.

Unscared, the daw, and starling nestle,
Where the tall turret rises high,
And winds alone come near to rustle
The thick leaves where their cradles lie.

I sometimes think, when late at even
I climb the stair reluctantly,
Some shape that should be well in heaven,
Or ill elsewhere, will pass by me.

I fear to see the very faces,
Familiar thirty years ago,
Even in the old accustomed places
Which look so cold and gloomy now.

I've come, to close the window, hither,
At twilight, when the sun was down,
And Fear, my very soul would wither,
Lest something should be dimly shown.

Too much the buried form resembling,
Of her who once was mistress here;
Lest doubtful shade, or moonbeam trembling,
Might take her aspect, once so dear.

Hers was this chamber; in her time
It seemed to me a pleasant room,
For then no cloud of grief or crime
Had cursed it with a settled gloom;

I had not seen death's image laid
In shroud and sheet, on yonder bed.
Before she married, she was blest –
Blest in her youth, blest in her worth;
Her mind was calm, its sunny rest
Shone in her eyes more clear than mirth.

And when attired in rich array,
Light, lustrous hair about her brow,
She yonder sat – a kind of day

Lit up – what seems so gloomy now.
These grim oak walls, even then were grim;
That old carved chair, was then antique;
But what around looked dusk and dim
Served as a foil to her fresh cheek;
Her neck, and arms, of hue so fair,
Eyes of unclouded, smiling, light;
Her soft, and curled, and floating hair,
Gems and attire, as rainbow bright.

Reclined in yonder deep recess,
Ofttimes she would, at evening, lie
Watching the sun; she seemed to bless
With happy glance the glorious sky.
She loved such scenes, and as she gazed,
Her face evinced her spirit's mood;
Beauty or grandeur ever raised
In her, a deep felt gratitude.

But of all lovely things, she loved
A cloudless moon, on summer night;
Full oft have I impatience proved
To see how long, her still delight
Would find a theme in reverie.
Out on the lawn, or where the trees
Let in the lustre fitfully,
As their boughs parted momently,
To the soft, languid, summer breeze.
Alas! that she should e'er have flung
Those pure, though lonely joys away –
Deceived by false and guileful tongue,
She gave her hand, then suffered wrong;
Oppressed, ill-used, she faded young,
And died of grief by slow decay.

Open that casket – look how bright
Those jewels flash upon the sight;
The brilliants have not lost a ray
Of lustre, since her wedding day.
But see – upon that pearly chain –

How dim lies time's discolouring stain!
I've seen that by her daughter worn:
For, e'er she died, a child was born;
A child that ne'er its mother knew,
That lone, and almost friendless grew;
For, ever, when its step drew nigh,
Averted was the father's eye;
And then, a life impure and wild
Made him a stranger to his child;
Absorbed in vice, he little cared
On what she did, or how she fared.

The love withheld, she never sought,
She grew uncherished – learnt untaught;
To her the inward life of thought
    Full soon was open laid.
I know not if her friendlessness
Did sometimes on her spirit press,
    But plaint she never made.
The book-shelves were her darling treasure,
She rarely seemed the time to measure
    While she could read alone.
And she too loved the twilight wood,
And often, in her mother's mood,
Away to yonder hill would hie,
Like her, to watch the setting sun,
Or see the stars born, one by one,
    Out of the darkening sky.
Nor would she leave that hill till night
Trembled from pole to pole with light;
Even then, upon her homeward way,
Long – long her wandering steps delayed
To quit the sombre forest shade,
Through which her eerie pathway lay.
You ask if she had beauty's grace?
I know not – but a nobler face
    My eyes have seldom seen;
A keen and fine intelligence,
And, better still, the truest sense
    Were in her speaking mien.

But bloom, or lustre was there none,
Only at moments, fitful shone
 An ardour in her eye,
That kindled on her cheek a flush,
Warm as a red sky's passing blush
 And quick with energy.
Her speech, too, was not common speech,
No wish to shine, or aim to teach,
 Was in her words displayed:
She still began with quiet sense,
But oft the force of eloquence
 Came to her lips in aid;
Language and voice unconscious changed,
And thoughts, in other words arranged,
 Her fervid soul transfused
Into the hearts of those who heard,
And transient strength and ardour stirred,
 In minds to strength unused.
Yet in gay crowd or festal glare,
Grave and retiring was her air;
'Twas seldom, save with me alone,
That fire of feeling freely shone;
She loved not awe's nor wonder's gaze,
Nor even exaggerated praise,
Nor even notice, if too keen
The curious gazer searched her mien.
Nature's own green expanse revealed
The world, the pleasures, she could prize;
On free hill-side, in sunny field,
In quiet spots by woods concealed,
Grew wild and fresh her chosen joys,
Yet Nature's feelings deeply lay
In that endowed and youthful frame;
Shrined in her heart and hid from day,
They burned unseen with silent flame;
In youth's first search for mental light,
She lived but to reflect and learn,
But soon her mind's maturer might
For stronger task did pant and yearn;
And stronger task did fate assign,

Task that a giant's strength might strain;
To suffer long and ne'er repine,
Be calm in frenzy, smile at pain.

Pale with the secret war of feeling,
Sustained with courage, mute, yet high;
The wounds at which she bled, revealing
Only by altered cheek and eye;

She bore in silence – but when passion
Surged in her soul with ceaseless foam,
The storm at last brought desolation,
And drove her exiled from her home.

And silent still, she straight assembled
The wrecks of strength her soul retained;
For though the wasted body trembled,
The unconquered mind, to quail, disdained.

She crossed the sea – now lone she wanders
By Seine's, or Rhine's, or Arno's flow;
Fain would I know if distance renders
Relief or comfort to her woe.

Fain would I know if, henceforth, ever,
These eyes shall read in hers again,
That light of love which faded never,
Though dimmed so long with secret pain.

She will return, but cold and altered,
Like all whose hopes too soon depart;
Like all on whom have beat, unsheltered,
The bitter blasts that blight the heart.

No more shall I behold her lying
Calm on a pillow, smoothed by me;
No more that spirit, worn with sighing,
Will know the rest of infancy.

If still the paths of lore she follow,
'Twill be with tired and goaded will;
She'll only toil, the aching hollow,
The joyless blank of life to fill.

And oh! full oft, quite spent and weary,
Her hand will pause, her head decline;
That labour seems so hard and dreary,
On which no ray of hope may shine.

Thus the pale blight of time and sorrow
Will shade with grey her soft, dark hair;
Then comes the day that knows no morrow,
And death succeeds to long despair.

So speaks experience, sage and hoary;
I see it plainly, know it well,
Like one who, having read a story,
Each incident therein can tell.

Touch not that ring, 'twas his, the sire
    Of that forsaken child;
And nought his relics can inspire
    Save memories, sin-defiled.

I, who sat by his wife's death-bed,
    I, who his daughter loved,
Could almost curse the guilty dead,
    For woes, the guiltless proved.

And heaven did curse – they found him laid,
    When crime for wrath was rife,
Cold – with the suicidal blade
    Clutched in his desperate gripe.

'Twas near that long deserted hut,
    Which in the wood decays,
Death's axe, self-wielded, struck his root,
    And lopped his desperate days.

You know the spot, where three black trees,
    Lift up their branches fell,
And moaning, ceaseless as the seas,
Still seem, in every passing breeze,
    The deed of blood to tell.

They named him mad, and laid his bones
    Where holier ashes lie;
Yet doubt not that his spirit groans,
    In hell's eternity.

But, lo! night, closing o'er the earth,
    Infects our thoughts with gloom;
Come, let us strive to rally mirth,
Where glows a clear and tranquil hearth
    In some more cheerful room.

CURRER

Stars

Ah! why, because the dazzling sun
    Restored our Earth to joy,
Have you departed, every one,
    And left a desert sky?

All through the night, your glorious eyes
    Were gazing down in mine,
And, with a full heart's thankful sighs,
    I blessed that watch divine.

I was at peace, and drank your beams
    As they were life to me;
And revelled in my changeful dreams,
    Like petrel on the sea.

Thought followed thought, star followed star,
    Through boundless regions, on;
While one sweet influence, near and far,
    Thrilled through, and proved us one!

Why did the morning dawn to break
    So great, so pure, a spell;
And scorch with fire, the tranquil cheek,
    Where your cool radiance fell?

Blood-red, he rose, and, arrow-straight,
    His fierce beams struck my brow;
The soul of nature, sprang, elate,
    But *mine* sank sad and low!

My lids closed down, yet through their veil,
    I saw him, blazing, still,
And steep in gold the misty dale,
    And flash upon the hill.

I turned me to the pillow, then,
    To call back night, and see
Your worlds of solemn light, again,
    Throb with my heart, and me!

It would not do – the pillow glowed,
    And glowed both roof and floor;
And birds sang loudly in the wood,
    And fresh winds shook the door;

The curtains waved, the wakened flies
    Were murmuring round my room,
Imprisoned there, till I should rise,
    And give them leave to roam.

Oh, stars, and dreams, and gentle night;
    Oh, night and stars return!
And hide me from the hostile light,
    That does not warm, but burn;

That drains the blood of suffering men;
    Drinks tears, instead of dew;
Let me sleep through his blinding reign,
    And only wake with you!

ELLIS

The Philosopher

'Enough of thought, philosopher!
　　Too long hast thou been dreaming
Unlightened, in this chamber drear,
　　While summer's sun is beaming!
Space-sweeping soul, what sad refrain
Concludes thy musings once again?

　　'Oh, for the time when I shall sleep
　　　Without identity,
　　And never care how rain may steep,
　　　Or snow may cover me!
　　No promised heaven, these wild desires,
　　　Could all, or half fulfil;
　　No threatened hell, with quenchless fires,
　　　Subdue this quenchless will!'

'So said I, and still say the same;
　　Still, to my death, will say –
Three gods, within this little frame,
　　Are warring night and day;
Heaven could not hold them all, and yet
　　They all are held in me;
And must be mine till I forget
　　My present entity!
Oh, for the time, when in my breast
　　Their struggles will be o'er!
Oh, for the day, when I shall rest,
　　And never suffer more!'

'I saw a spirit, standing, man,
　　Where thou dost stand – an hour ago,
And round his feet three rivers ran,
　　Of equal depth, and equal flow –
A golden stream – and one like blood;
　　And one like sapphire seemed to be;
But, where they joined their triple flood
　　It tumbled in an inky sea.

The spirit sent his dazzling gaze
   Down through that ocean's gloomy night
Then, kindling all, with sudden blaze,
   The glad deep sparkled wide and bright –
White as the sun, far, far more fair
   Than its divided sources were!'

'And even for that spirit, seer,
   I've watched and sought my life-time long;
Sought him in heaven, hell, earth, and air –
   An endless search, and always wrong!
Had I but seen his glorious eye
   Once light the clouds that wilder me,
I ne'er had raised this coward cry
   To cease to think, and cease to be;
I ne'er had called oblivion blest,
   Nor, stretching eager hands to death,
Implored to change for senseless rest
   This sentient soul, this living breath –
Oh, let me die – that power and will
   Their cruel strife may close;
And conquered good, and conquering ill
   Be lost in one repose!'

ELLIS

The Arbour

I'll rest me in this sheltered bower,
And look upon the clear blue sky
That smiles upon me through the trees,
Which stand so thickly clustering by;

And view their green and glossy leaves,
All glistening in the sunshine fair;
And list the rustling of their boughs,
So softly whispering through the air.

And while my ear drinks in the sound,
My winged soul shall fly away;
Reviewing long departed years
As one mild, beaming, autumn day;

And soaring on to future scenes,
Like hills and woods, and valleys green,
All basking in the summer's sun,
But distant still, and dimly seen.

Oh, list! 'tis summer's very breath
That gently shakes the rustling trees –
But look! the snow is on the ground –
How can I think of scenes like these?

'Tis but the *frost* that clears the air,
And gives the sky that lovely blue;
They're smiling in a *winter*'s sun,
Those evergreens of sombre hue.

And winter's chill is on my heart –
How can I dream of future bliss?
How can my spirit soar away,
Confined by such a chain as this?

ACTON

Home

How brightly glistening in the sun
   The woodland ivy plays!
While yonder beeches from their barks
   Reflect his silver rays.

That sun surveys a lovely scene
   From softly smiling skies;
And wildly through unnumbered trees
   The wind of winter sighs:

Now loud, it thunders o'er my head,
   And now in distance dies.
But give me back my barren hills
   Where colder breezes rise;

Where scarce the scattered, stunted trees
   Can yield an answering swell,
But where a wilderness of heath
   Returns the sound as well.

For yonder garden, fair and wide,
   With groves of evergreen,
Long winding walks, and borders trim,
   And velvet lawns between;

Restore to me that little spot,
   With grey walls compassed round,
Where knotted grass neglected lies,
   And weeds usurp the ground.

Though all around this mansion high
   Invites the foot to roam,
And though its halls are fair within –
   Oh, give me back my HOME!

ACTON

The Wife's Will

Sit still – a word – a breath may break
(As light airs stir a sleeping lake,)
The glassy calm that soothes my woes,
The sweet, the deep, the full repose.

O leave me not! for ever be
Thus, more than life itself to me!

Yes, close beside thee, let me kneel –
Give me thy hand that I may feel
The friend so true – so tried – so dear,
My heart's own chosen – indeed is near;
And check me not – this hour divine
Belongs to me – is fully mine.

'Tis thy own hearth thou sitt'st beside,
After long absence – wandering wide;
'Tis thy own wife reads in thine eyes,
A promise clear of stormless skies,
For faith and true love light the rays,
Which shine responsive to her gaze.

Aye, – well that single tear may fall;
Ten thousand might mine eyes recall,
Which from their lids, ran blinding fast,
In hours of grief, yet scarcely past,
Well may'st thou speak of love to me;
For, oh! most truly – I love thee!

Yet smile – for we are happy now.
Whence, then, that sadness on thy brow?
What say'st thou? 'We must once again,
Ere long, be severed by the main?'
I knew not this – I deemed no more,
Thy step would err from Britain's shore.

'Duty commands?' 'Tis true – 'tis just;
Thy slightest word I wholly trust,
Nor by request, nor faintest sigh
Would I, to turn thy purpose, try;
But, William – hear my solemn vow –
Hear and confirm! – with thee I go.

'Distance and suffering,' did'st thou say?
'Danger by night, and toil by day?'
Oh, idle words, and vain are these;
Hear me! I cross with thee the seas.
Such risk as thou must meet and dare,
I – thy true wife – will duly share.

Passive, at home, I will not pine;
Thy toils – thy perils, shall be mine;
Grant this – and be hereafter paid
By a warm heart's devoted aid:
'Tis granted – with that yielding kiss,
Entered my soul unmingled bliss.

Thanks, William – thanks! thy love has joy,
Pure – undefiled with base alloy;
'Tis not a passion, false and blind,
Inspires, enchains, absorbs my mind;
Worthy, I feel, art thou to be
Loved with my perfect energy.

This evening, now, shall sweetly flow,
Lit by our clear fire's happy glow;
And parting's peace-embittering fear,
Is warned, our hearts to come not near;
For fate admits my soul's decree,
In bliss or bale – to go with thee!

CURRER

Remembrance

Cold in the earth – and the deep snow piled above thee,
Far, far, removed, cold in the dreary grave!
Have I forgot, my only Love, to love thee,
Severed at last by Time's all-severing wave?

Now, when alone, do my thoughts no longer hover
Over the mountains, on that northern shore,
Resting their wings where heath and fern-leaves cover
Thy noble heart for ever, ever more?

Cold in the earth – and fifteen wild Decembers,
From those brown hills, have melted into spring:
Faithful, indeed, is the spirit that remembers
After such years of change and suffering!

Sweet Love of youth, forgive, if I forget thee,
While the world's tide is bearing me along;
Other desires and other hopes beset me,
Hopes which obscure, but cannot do thee wrong!

No later light has lightened up my heaven,
No second morn has ever shone for me;
All my life's bliss from thy dear life was given,
All my life's bliss is in the grave with thee.

But, when the days of golden dreams had perished,
And even Despair was powerless to destroy;
Then did I learn how existence could be cherished,
Strengthened, and fed without the aid of joy.

Then did I check the tears of useless passion –
Weaned my young soul from yearning after thine;
Sternly denied its burning wish to hasten
Down to that tomb already more than mine.

And, even yet, I dare not let it languish,
Dare not indulge in memory's rapturous pain;
Once drinking deep of that divinest anguish,
How could I seek the empty world again?

ELLIS

Vanitas Vanitatum, Omnia Vanitas

In all we do, and hear, and see,
Is restless Toil and Vanity.
While yet thc rolling earth abides,
Men come and go like ocean tides;

And ere one generation dies,
Another in its place shall rise;
That, sinking soon into the grave,
Others succeed, like wave on wave;

And as they rise, they pass away.
The sun arises every day,
And, hastening onward to the West,
He nightly sinks, but not to rest:

Returning to the eastern skies,
Again to light us, he must rise.
And still the restless wind comes forth,
Now blowing keenly from the North;

Now from the South, the East, the West,
For ever changing, ne'er at rest.
The fountains, gushing from the hills,
Supply the ever-running rills;

The thirsty rivers drink their store,
And bear it rolling to the shore,
But still the ocean craves for more.
'Tis endless labour everywhere!
Sound cannot satisfy the ear,

Light cannot fill the craving eye,
Nor riches half our wants supply;
Pleasure but doubles future pain,
And joy brings sorrow in her train;

Laughter is mad, and reckless mirth –
What does she in this weary earth?
Should Wealth, or Fame, our Life employ,
Death comes, our labour to destroy;

To snatch the untasted cup away,
For which we toiled so many a day.
What, then, remains for wretched man?
To use life's comforts while he can,

Enjoy the blessings Heaven bestows,
Assist his friends, forgive his foes;
Trust God, and keep his statutes still,
Upright and firm, through good and ill;

Thankful for all that God has given,
Fixing his firmest hopes on heaven;
Knowing that earthly joys decay,
But hoping through the darkest day.

ACTON

The Wood

But two miles more, and then we rest!
Well, there is still an hour of day,
And long the brightness of the West
Will light us on our devious way;
Sit then, awhile, here in this wood –
So total is the solitude,
    We safely may delay.

These massive roots afford a seat,
Which seems for weary travellers made.
There rest. The air is soft and sweet
In this sequestered forest glade,
And there are scents of flowers around,
The evening dew draws from the ground;
    How soothingly they spread!

Yes; I was tired, but not at heart;
No – that beats full of sweet content,
For now I have my natural part
Of action with adventure blent;
Cast forth on the wide world with thee.
And all my once waste energy
    To weighty purpose bent.

Yet – say'st thou, spies around us roam.
Our aims are termed conspiracy?
Haply, no more our English home
An anchorage for us may be?
That there is risk our mutual blood
May redden in some lonely wood
    The knife of treachery?

Say'st thou – that where we lodge each night,
In each lone farm, or lonelier hall
Of Norman Peer – ere morning light
Suspicion must as duly fall,
As day returns – such vigilance
Presides and watches over France,
       Such rigour governs all?

I fear not, William; dost thou fear?
So that the knife does not divide,
It may be ever hovering near:
I could not tremble at thy side,
And strenuous love – like mine for thee –
Is buckler strong, 'gainst treachery,
       And turns its stab aside.

I am resolved that thou shalt learn
To trust my strength as I trust thine;
I am resolved our souls shall burn,
With equal, steady, mingling shine;
Part of the field is conquered now,
Our lives in the same channel flow,
       Along the self-same line;

And while no groaning storm is heard,
Thou seem'st content it should be so,
But soon as comes a warning word
Of danger – straight thine anxious brow
Bends over me a mournful shade,
As doubting if my powers are made
       To ford the floods of woe.

Know, then it is my spirit swells,
And drinks, with eager joy, the air
Of freedom – where at last it dwells,
Chartered, a common task to share
With thee, and then it stirs alert,
And pants to learn what menaced hurt
       Demands for thee its care.

Remember, I have crossed the deep,
And stood with thee on deck, to gaze
On waves that rose in threatening heap,
While stagnant lay a heavy haze,
Dimly confusing sea with sky,
And baffling, even, the pilot's eye,
    Intent to thread the maze –

Of rocks, on Bretagne's dangerous coast,
And find a way to steer our band
To the one point obscure, which lost,
Flung us, as victims, on the strand; –
All, elsewhere, gleamed the Gallic sword,
And not a wherry could be moored
    Along the guarded land.

I feared not then – I fear not now;
The interest of each stirring scene
Wakes a new sense, a welcome glow,
In every nerve and bounding vein;
Alike on turbid Channel sea,
Or in still wood of Normandy,
    I feel as born again.

The rain descended that wild morn
When, anchoring in the cove at last,
Our band, all weary and forlorn,
Ashore, like wave-worn sailors, cast –
Sought for a sheltering roof in vain,
And scarce could scanty food obtain
    To break their morning fast.

Thou didst thy crust with me divide,
Thou didst thy cloak around me fold;
And, sitting silent by thy side,
I ate the bread in peace untold:
Given kindly from thy hand, 'twas sweet
As costly fare or princely treat
    On royal plate of gold.

Sharp blew the sleet upon my face,
And, rising wild, the gusty wind
Drove on those thundering waves apace,
Our crew so late had left behind;
But, spite of frozen shower and storm,
So close to thee, my heart beat warm,
      And tranquil slept my mind.

So now – nor foot-sore nor opprest
With walking all this August day,
I taste a heaven in this brief rest,
This gypsy-halt beside the way.
England's wild flowers are fair to view,
Like balm is England's summer dew,
      Like gold her sunset ray.

But the white violets, growing here,
Are sweeter than I yet have seen,
And ne'er did dew so pure and clear
Distil on forest mosses green,
As now, called forth by summer heat,
Perfumes our cool and fresh retreat –
      These fragrant limes between.

That sunset! Look beneath the boughs,
Over the copse – beyond the hills;
How soft, yet deep and warm it glows,
And heaven with rich suffusion fills;
With hues where still the opal's tint,
Its gleam of prisoned fire is blent,
      Where flame through azure thrills!

Depart we now – for fast will fade
That solemn splendour of decline,
And deep must be the after-shade
As stars alone tonight will shine;
No moon is destined – pale – to gaze
On such a day's vast Phœnix blaze,
      A day in fires decayed!

There – hand-in-hand we tread again
The mazes of this varying wood,
And soon, amid a cultured plain,
Girt in with fertile solitude,
We shall our resting-place descry,
Marked by one roof-tree, towering high
        Above a farm-stead rude.

Refreshed, erelong, with rustic fare,
We'll seek a couch of dreamless ease;
Courage will guard thy heart from fear,
And Love give mine divinest peace:
Tomorrow brings more dangerous toil,
And through its conflict and turmoil
        We'll pass, as God shall please.

                                    CURRER

A Death Scene

'O Day! he cannot die
When thou so fair art shining!
O Sun, in such a glorious sky,
So tranquilly declining;

He cannot leave thee now,
While fresh west winds are blowing,
And all around his youthful brow
Thy cheerful light is glowing!

Edward, awake, awake –
The golden evening gleams
Warm and bright on Arden's lake –
Arouse thee from thy dreams!

Beside thee, on my knee,
My dearest friend! I pray
That thou, to cross the eternal sea,
Wouldst yet one hour delay:

I hear its billows roar –
I see them foaming high;
But no glimpse of a further shore
Has blest my straining eye.

Believe not what they urge
Of Eden isles beyond;
Turn back, from that tempestuous surge,
To thy own native land.

It is not death, but pain
That struggles in thy breast –
Nay, rally, Edward, rouse again;
I cannot let thee rest!'

One long look, that sore reproved me
For the woe I could not bear –
One mute look of suffering moved me
To repent my useless prayer:

And, with sudden check, the heaving
Of distraction passed away;
Not a sign of further grieving
Stirred my soul that awful day.

Paled, at length, the sweet sun setting;
Sunk to peace the twilight breeze:
Summer dews fell softly, wetting
Glen, and glade, and silent trees.

Then his eyes began to weary,
Weighed beneath a mortal sleep;
And their orbs grew strangely dreary,
Clouded, even as they would weep.

But they wept not, but they changed not,
Never moved, and never closed;
Troubled still, and still they ranged not –
Wandered not, nor yet reposed!

So I knew that he was dying –
Stooped, and raised his languid head;
Felt no breath, and heard no sighing,
So I knew that he was dead.

ELLIS

Song

The linnet in the rocky dells,
    The moor-lark in the air,
The bee among the heather bells,
    That hide my lady fair:

The wild deer browse above her breast;
    The wild birds raise their brood;
And they, her smiles of love caressed,
    Have left her solitude!

I ween, that when the grave's dark wall
    Did first her form retain;
They thought their hearts could ne'er recall
    The light of joy again.

They thought the tide of grief would flow
    Unchecked through future years;
But where is all their anguish now,
    And where are all their tears?

Well, let them fight for honour's breath,
    Or pleasure's shade pursue –
The dweller in the land of death
    Is changed and careless too.

And, if their eyes should watch and weep
    Till sorrow's source were dry,
She would not, in her tranquil sleep,
    Return a single sigh!

Blow, west-wind, by the lonely mound,
    And murmur, summer-streams –
There is no need of other sound
    To soothe my lady's dreams.

ELLIS

The Penitent

I mourn with thee, and yet rejoice
    That thou shouldst sorrow so;
With angel choirs I join my voice
    To bless the sinner's woe.

Though friends and kindred turn away,
    And laugh thy grief to scorn;
I hear the great Redeemer say,
    'Blessed are ye that mourn.'

Hold on thy course, nor deem it strange
    That earthly cords are riven:
Man may lament the wondrous change,
    But 'there is joy in heaven!'

ACTON

Music on Christmas Morning

Music I love – but never strain
Could kindle raptures so divine,
So grief assuage, so conquer pain,
And rouse this pensive heart of mine –
As that we hear on Christmas morn,
Upon the wintry breezes borne.

Though Darkness still her empire keep,
And hours must pass, ere morning break;
From troubled dreams, or slumbers deep,
That music *kindly* bids us wake:
It calls us, with an angel's voice,
To wake, and worship, and rejoice;

To greet with joy the glorious morn,
Which angels welcomed long ago,
When our redeeming Lord was born,
To bring the light of Heaven below;
The Powers of Darkness to dispel,
And rescue Earth from Death and Hell.

While listening to that sacred strain,
My raptured spirit soars on high;
I seem to hear those songs again
Resounding through the open sky,
That kindled such divine delight,
In those who watched their flocks by night.

With them, I celebrate His birth –
Glory to God, in highest Heaven,
Good will to men, and peace on Earth,
To us a Saviour-king is given;
Our God is come to claim His own,
And Satan's power is overthrown!

A sinless God, for sinful men,
Descends to suffer and to bleed;
Hell *must* renounce its empire then;
The price is paid, the world is freed.
And Satan's self must now confess,
That Christ has earned a *Right* to bless:

Now holy Peace may smile from heaven,
And heavenly Truth from earth shall spring:
The captive's galling bonds are riven,
For our Redeemer is our king;
And He that gave his blood for men
Will lead us home to God again.

ACTON

Frances

She will not sleep, for fear of dreams,
But, rising, quits her restless bed,
And walks where some beclouded beams
Of moonlight through the hall are shed.

Obedient to the goad of grief,
Her steps, now fast, now lingering slow,
In varying motion seek relief
From the Eumenides of woe.

Wringing her hands, at intervals –
But long as mute as phantom dim –
She glides along the dusky walls,
Under the black oak rafters, grim.

The close air of the grated tower
Stifles a heart that scarce can beat,
And, though so late and lone the hour,
Forth pass her wandering, faltering feet;

And on the pavement, spread before
The long front of the mansion grey,
Her steps imprint the night-frost hoar,
Which pale on grass and granite lay.

Not long she stayed where misty moon
And shimmering stars could on her look,
But through the garden arch-way, soon
Her strange and gloomy path she took.

Some firs, coeval with the tower,
Their straight black boughs stretched o'er her head,
Unseen, beneath this sable bower,
Rustled her dress and rapid tread.

There was an alcove in that shade,
Screening a rustic-seat and stand;
Weary she sat her down and laid
Her hot brow on her burning hand.

To solitude and to the night,
Some words she now, in murmurs, said;
And, trickling through her fingers white,
Some tears of misery she shed.

'God help me, in my grievous need,
God help me, in my inward pain;
Which cannot ask for pity's meed,
Which has no license to complain;

Which must be borne, yet who can bear,
Hours long, days long, a constant weight –
The yoke of absolute despair,
A suffering wholly desolate?

Who can for ever crush the heart,
Restrain its throbbing, curb its life?
Dissemble truth with ceaseless art,
With outward calm, mask inward strife?'

She waited – as for some reply;
The still and cloudy night gave none;
Erelong, with deep-drawn, trembling sigh,
Her heavy plaint again begun.

'Unloved – I love; unwept – I weep;
Grief I restrain – hope I repress:
Vain is this anguish – fixed and deep;
Vainer, desires and dreams of bliss.

My love awakes no love again,
My tears collect, and fall unfelt;
My sorrow touches none with pain,
My humble hopes to nothing melt.

For me the universe is dumb,
Stone-deaf, and blank, and wholly blind;
Life I must bound, existence sum
In the strait limits of one mind;

That mind my own. Oh! narrow cell;
Dark – imageless – a living tomb!
There must I sleep, there wake and dwell
Content, with palsy, pain, and gloom.'

Again she paused; a moan of pain,
A stifled sob, alone was heard;
Long silence followed – then again,
Her voice the stagnant midnight stirred.

'Must it be so? Is this my fate?
Can I nor struggle, nor contend?
And am I doomed for years to wait,
Watching death's lingering axe descend?

And when it falls, and when I die,
What follows? Vacant nothingness?
The blank of lost identity?
Erasure both of pain and bliss?

I've heard of heaven – I would believe;
For if this earth indeed be all,
Who longest lives may deepest grieve,
Most blest, whom sorrows soonest call.

Oh! leaving disappointment here,
Will man find hope on yonder coast?
Hope, which, on earth, shines never clear,
And oft in clouds is wholly lost.

Will he hope's source of light behold,
Fruition's spring, where doubts expire,
And drink, in waves of living gold,
Contentment, full, for long desire?

Will he find bliss, which here he dreamed?
Rest, which was weariness on earth?
Knowledge, which, if o'er life it beamed,
Served but to prove it void of worth?

Will he find love without lust's leaven,
Love fearless, tearless, perfect, pure,
To all with equal bounty given,
In all, unfeigned, unfailing, sure?

Will he, from penal sufferings free,
Released from shroud and wormy clod,
All calm and glorious, rise and see
Creation's Sire – Existence' God?

Then, glancing back on Time's brief woes,
Will he behold them, fading, fly;
Swept from Eternity's repose,
Like sullying cloud, from pure blue sky?

If so – endure, my weary frame;
And when thy anguish strikes too deep,
And when all troubled burns life's flame,
Think of the quiet, final sleep;

Think of the glorious waking-hour,
Which will not dawn on grief and tears,
But on a ransomed spirit's power,
Certain, and free from mortal fears.

Seek now thy couch, and lie till morn,
Then from thy chamber, calm, descend,
With mind nor tossed, nor anguish-torn,
But tranquil, fixed, to wait the end.

And when thy opening eyes shall see
Mementos, on the chamber wall,
Of one who has forgotten thee,
Shed not the tear of acrid gall.

The tear which, welling from the heart,
Burns where its drop corrosive falls,
And makes each nerve, in torture, start,
At feelings it too well recalls:

When the sweet hope of being loved,
Threw Eden sunshine on life's way;
When every sense and feeling proved
Expectancy of brightest day.

When the hand trembled to receive
A thrilling clasp, which seemed so near,
And the heart ventured to believe,
Another heart esteemed it dear.

When words, half love, all tenderness,
Were hourly heard, as hourly spoken,
When the long, sunny days of bliss,
Only by moonlight nights were broken.

Till drop by drop, the cup of joy
Filled full, with purple light, was glowing,
And Faith, which watched it, sparkling high,
Still never dreamt the overflowing.

It fell not with a sudden crashing,
It poured not out like open sluice;
No, sparkling still, and redly flashing,
Drained, drop by drop, the generous juice.

I saw it sink, and strove to taste it,
My eager lips approached the brim;
The movement only seemed to waste it,
It sank to dregs, all harsh and dim.

These I have drunk, and they for ever
Have poisoned life and love for me;
A draught from Sodom's lake could never
More fiery, salt, and bitter, be.

Oh! Love was all a thin illusion;
Joy, but the desert's flying stream;
And, glancing back on long delusion,
My memory grasps a hollow dream.

Yet, whence that wondrous change of feeling,
I never knew, and cannot learn,
Nor why my lover's eye, congealing,
Drew cold, and clouded, proud, and stern.

Nor wherefore, friendship's forms forgetting,
He careless left, and cool withdrew;
Nor spoke of grief, nor fond regretting,
Nor even one glance of comfort threw.

And neither word nor token sending,
Of kindness, since the parting day,
His course, for distant regions bending,
Went, self-contained and calm, away.

Oh, bitter, blighting, keen sensation,
Which will not weaken, cannot die,
Hasten thy work of desolation,
And let my tortured spirit fly!

Vain as the passing gale, my crying;
Though lightning-struck, I must live on;
I know, at heart, there is no dying
Of love, and ruined hope, alone.

Still strong, and young, and warm with vigour,
Though scathed, I long shall greenly grow,
And many a storm of wildest rigour
Shall yet break o'er my shivered bough.

Rebellious now to blank inertion,
My unused strength demands a task;
Travel, and toil, and full exertion,
Are the last, only boon I ask.

Whence, then, this vain and barren dreaming
Of death, and dubious life to come?
I see a nearer beacon gleaming
Over dejection's sea of gloom.

The very wildness of my sorrow
Tells me I yet have innate force;
My track of life has been too narrow,
Effort shall trace a broader course.

The world is not in yonder tower,
Earth is not prisoned in that room,
'Mid whose dark pannels, hour by hour,
I've sat, the slave and prey of gloom.

One feeling – turned to utter anguish,
Is not my being's only aim;
When, lorn and loveless, life will languish,
But courage can revive the flame.

He, when he left me, went a roving
To sunny climes, beyond the sea;
And I, the weight of woe removing,
Am free and fetterless as he.

New scenes, new language, skies less clouded.
May once more wake the wish to live;
Strange, foreign towns, astir, and crowded,
New pictures to the mind may give.

New forms and faces, passing ever,
May hide the one I still retain,
Defined, and fixed, and fading never,
Stamped deep on vision, heart, and brain.

And we might meet – time may have changed him;
Chance may reveal the mystery,
The secret influence which estranged him;
Love may restore him yet to me.

False thought – false hope – in scorn be banished!
I am not loved – nor loved have been;
Recall not, then, the dreams scarce vanished,
Traitors! mislead me not again!

To words like yours I bid defiance,
'Tis such my mental wreck have made;
Of God alone, and self-reliance,
I ask for solace – hope for aid.

Morn comes – and ere meridian glory
O'er these, my natal woods, shall smile,
Both lonely wood and mansion hoary
I'll leave behind, full many a mile.

CURRER

Anticipation

How beautiful the earth is still,
To thee – how full of happiness!
How little fraught with real ill,
Or unreal phantoms of distress!
How spring can bring thee glory, yet,
And summer win thee to forget
December's sullen time!
Why dost thou hold the treasure fast,
Of youth's delight, when youth is past,
    And thou art near thy prime?

When those who were thy own compeers,
Equals in fortune and in years,
Have seen their morning melt in tears,
    To clouded, smileless day;
Blest, had they died untried and young,
Before their hearts went wandering wrong,
Poor slaves, subdued by passions strong,
    A weak and helpless prey!

'Because, I hoped while they enjoyed,
And, by fulfilment, hope destroyed;
As children hope, with trustful breast,
I waited bliss – and cherished rest.
A thoughtful spirit taught me, soon,
That we must long till life be done;
That every phase of earthly joy
Must always fade, and always cloy:

This I foresaw – and would not chase
    The fleeting treacheries;
But, with firm foot and tranquil face,
Held backward from that tempting race,
Gazed o'er the sands the waves efface,
    To the enduring seas –

There cast my anchor of desire
Deep in unknown eternity;
Nor ever let my spirit tire,
With looking for *what is to be!*

It is hope's spell that glorifies,
Like youth, to my maturer eyes,
All Nature's million mysteries,
    The fearful and the fair –
Hope soothes me in the griefs I know;
She lulls my pain for others' woe,
And makes me strong to undergo
    What I am born to bear.

Glad comforter! will I not brave,
Unawed, the darkness of the grave?
Nay, smile to hear Death's billows rave –
    Sustained, my guide, by thee?
The more unjust seems present fate,
The more my spirit swells elate,
Strong, in thy strength, to anticipate
    Rewarding destiny!'

                                        ELLIS

Stanzas

Oh, weep not, love! each tear that springs
    In those dear eyes of thine,
To me a keener suffering brings,
    Than if they flowed from mine.

And do not droop! however drear
    The fate awaiting thee;
For *my* sake combat pain and care,
    And cherish life for me!

I do not fear thy love will fail;
    Thy faith is true, I know;
But, oh, my love! thy strength is frail
    For such a life of woe.

Were't not for this, I well could trace
    (Though banished long from thee,)
Life's rugged path, and boldly face
    The storms that threaten me.

Fear not for me – I've steeled my mind
    Sorrow and strife to greet;
Joy with my love I leave behind,
    Care with my friends I meet.

A mother's sad reproachful eye,
    A father's scowling brow –
But he may frown and she may sigh:
    I will not break my vow!

I love my mother, I revere
    My sire, but fear not me –
Believe that Death alone can tear
    This faithful heart from thee.

ACTON

Gilbert

I

THE GARDEN

Above the city hung the moon,
    Right o'er a plot of ground
Where flowers and orchard-trees were fenced
    With lofty walls around:
'Twas Gilbert's garden – there, tonight
    Awhile he walked alone;
And, tired with sedentary toil,
    Mused where the moonlight shone.

This garden, in a city-heart,
    Lay still as houseless wild,
Though many-windowed mansion fronts
    Were round it closely piled;
But thick their walls, and those within
    Lived lives by noise unstirred;
Like wafting of an angel's wing,
    Time's flight by them was heard.

Some soft piano-notes alone
    Were sweet as faintly given,
Where ladies, doubtless, cheered the hearth
    With song, that winter-even.
The city's many-mingled sounds
    Rose like the hum of ocean;
They rather lulled the heart than roused
    Its pulse to faster motion.

Gilbert has paced the single walk
    An hour, yet is not weary;
And, though it be a winter night,
    He feels nor cold nor dreary.
The prime of life is in his veins,
    And sends his blood fast flowing,
And Fancy's fervour warms the thoughts
    Now in his bosom glowing.

Those thoughts recur to early love,
  Or what he love would name,
Though haply Gilbert's secret deeds
  Might other title claim.
Such theme not oft his mind absorbs,
  He to the world clings fast,
And too much for the present lives,
  To linger o'er the past.

But now the evening's deep repose
  Has glided to his soul;
That moonlight falls on Memory,
  And shows her fading scroll.
One name appears in every line
  The gentle rays shine o'er,
And still he smiles and still repeats
  That one name – Elinor.

There is no sorrow in his smile,
  No kindness in his tone;
The triumph of a selfish heart
  Speaks coldly there alone;
He says: 'She loved me more than life;
  And truly it was sweet
To see so fair a woman kneel,
  In bondage, at my feet.

There was a sort of quiet bliss
  To be so deeply loved,
To gaze on trembling eagerness
  And sit myself unmoved.
And when it pleased my pride to grant,
  At last some rare caress,
To feel the fever of that hand
  My fingers deigned to press.

'Twas sweet to see her strive to hide
    What every glance revealed;
Endowed, the while, with despot-might
    Her destiny to wield.
I knew myself no perfect man,
    Nor, as she deemed, divine;
I knew that I was glorious – but
    By her reflected shine;

Her youth, her native energy,
    Her powers new-born and fresh,
'Twas these with Godhead sanctified
    My sensual frame of flesh.
Yet, like a god did I descend
    At last, to meet her love;
And, like a god, I then withdrew
    To my own heaven above.

And never more could she invoke
    My presence to her sphere;
No prayer, no plaint, no cry of hers
    Could win my awful ear.
I knew her blinded constancy
    Would ne'er my deeds betray,
And, calm in conscience, whole in heart,
    I went my tranquil way.

Yet, sometimes, I still feel a wish,
    The fond and flattering pain
Of passion's anguish to create,
    In her young breast again.
Bright was the lustre of her eyes,
    When they caught fire from mine;
If I had power – this very hour,
    Again I'd light their shine.

But where she is, or how she lives,
   I have no clue to know;
I've heard she long my absence pined,
   And left her home in woe.
But busied, then, in gathering gold,
   As I am busied now,
I could not turn from such pursuit,
   To weep a broken vow.

Nor could I give to fatal risk
   The fame I ever prized;
Even now, I fear, that precious fame
   Is too much compromised.'
An inward trouble dims his eye,
   Some riddle he would solve;
Some method to unloose a knot,
   His anxious thoughts revolve.

He, pensive, leans against a tree,
   A leafy evergreen,
The boughs, the moonlight, intercept,
   And hide him like a screen;
He starts – the tree shakes with his tremor,
   Yet nothing near him pass'd,
He hurries up the garden alley,
   In strangely sudden haste.

With shaking hand, he lifts the latchet,
   Steps o'er the threshold stone;
The heavy door slips from his fingers,
   It shuts, and he is gone.
What touched, transfixed, appalled, his soul?
   A nervous thought, no more;
'Twill sink like stone in placid pool,
   And calm close smoothly o'er.

II

THE PARLOUR

Warm is the parlour atmosphere,
  Serene the lamp's soft light;
The vivid embers, red and clear,
  Proclaim a frosty night.
Books, varied, on the table lie,
  Three children o'er them bend,
And all, with curious, eager eye,
  The turning leaf attend.

Picture and tale alternately
  Their simple hearts delight,
And interest deep, and tempered glee,
  Illume their aspects bright;
The parents, from their fireside place,
  Behold that pleasant scene,
And joy is on the mother's face,
  Pride, in the father's mien.

As Gilbert sees his blooming wife,
  Beholds his children fair,
No thought has he of transient strife,
  Or past, though piercing fear.
The voice of happy infancy
  Lisps sweetly in his ear,
His wife, with pleased and peaceful eye,
  Sits, kindly smiling, near.

The fire glows on her silken dress,
  And shows its ample grace,
And warmly tints each hazel tress,
  Curled soft around her face.
The beauty that in youth he wooed,
  Is beauty still, unfaded,
The brow of ever placid mood
  No churlish grief has shaded.

Prosperity, in Gilbert's home,
 Abides, the guest of years;
There Want or Discord never come,
 And seldom Toil or Tears.
The carpets bear the peaceful print
 Of comfort's velvet tread,
And golden gleams from plenty sent,
 In every nook are shed.

The very silken spaniel seems
 Of quiet ease to tell,
As near its mistress' feet it dreams,
 Sunk in a cushion's swell;
And smiles seem native to the eyes
 Of those sweet children, three;
They have but looked on tranquil skies,
 And know not misery.

Alas! that misery should come
 In such an hour as this;
Why could she not so calm a home
 A little longer miss?
But she is now within the door,
 Her steps advancing glide;
Her sullen shade has crossed the floor,
 She stands at Gilbert's side.

She lays her hand upon his heart,
 It bounds with agony;
His fireside chair shakes with the start
 That shook the garden tree.
His wife towards the children looks,
 She does not mark his mien;
The children, bending o'er their books,
 His terror have not seen.

In his own home, by his own hearth,
    He sits in solitude,
And circled round with light and mirth,
    Cold horror chills his blood.
His mind would hold with desperate clutch
    The scene that round him lies;
No – changed, as by some wizard's touch,
    The present prospect flies.

A tumult vague – a viewless strife
    His futile struggles crush;
'Twixt him and his, an unknown life
    And unknown feelings rush.
He sees – but scarce can language paint
    The tissue Fancy weaves;
For words oft give but echo faint
    Of thoughts the mind conceives.

Noise, tumult strange, and darkness dim,
    Efface both light and quiet;
No shape is in those shadows grim,
    No voice in that wild riot.
Sustained and strong, a wondrous blast
    Above and round him blows;
A greenish gloom, dense overcast,
    Each moment denser grows.

He nothing knows – nor clearly sees,
    Resistance checks his breath,
The high, impetuous, ceaseless breeze
    Blows on him, cold as death.
And still the undulating gloom
    Mocks sight with formless motion;
Was such sensation Jonah's doom,
    Gulphed in the depths of ocean?

Streaking the air, the nameless vision,
    Fast-driven, deep-sounding, flows;
Oh! whence its source, and what its mission?
    How will its terrors close?
Long-sweeping, rushing, vast and void,
    The Universe it swallows;
And still the dark, devouring tide,
    A Typhoon tempest follows.

More slow it rolls; its furious race
    Sinks to a solemn gliding;
The stunning roar, the wind's wild chase,
    To stillness are subsiding.
And, slowly borne along, a form
    The shapeless chaos varies;
Poised in the eddy of the storm,
    Before the eye it tarries.

A woman drowned – sunk in the deep,
    On a long wave reclining;
The circling waters' crystal sweep,
    Like glass, her shape enshrining;
Her pale dead face, to Gilbert turned,
    Seems as in sleep reposing;
A feeble light, now first discerned,
    The features well disclosing.

No effort from the haunted air
    The ghastly scene could banish;
That hovering wave, arrested there,
    Rolled – throbbed – but did not vanish.
If Gilbert upward turned his gaze,
    He saw the ocean-shadow;
If he looked down, the endless seas
    Lay green as summer meadow.

And straight before, the pale corpse lay,
    Upborne by air or billow,
So near, he could have touched the spray
    That churned around its pillow.
The hollow anguish of the face
    Had moved a fiend to sorrow;
Not Death's fixed calm could rase the trace
    Of suffering's deep-worn furrow.

All moved; a strong returning blast,
    The mass of waters raising,
Bore wave and passive carcase past,
    While Gilbert yet was gazing.
Deep in her isle-conceiving womb,
    It seemed the Ocean thundered,
And soon, by realms of rushing gloom,
    Were seer and phantom sundered.

Then swept some timbers from a wreck,
    On following surges riding;
Then sea-weed, in the turbid rack
    Uptorn, went slowly gliding.
The horrid shade, by slow degrees,
    A beam of light defeated,
And then the roar of raving seas,
    Fast, far, and faint, retreated.

And all was gone — gone like a mist,
    Corse, billows, tempest, wreck;
Three children close to Gilbert prest
    And clung around his neck.
Good night! good night! the prattlers said
    And kissed their father's cheek;
'Twas now the hour their quiet bed
    And placid rest to seek.

The mother with her offspring goes
    To hear their evening prayer;
She nought of Gilbert's vision knows,
    And nought of his despair.
Yet, pitying God, abridge the time
    Of anguish, now his fate!
Though, haply, great has been his crime,
    Thy mercy, too, is great.

Gilbert, at length, uplifts his head,
 Bent for some moments low,
And there is neither grief nor dread
Upon his subtle brow.
For well can he his feelings task,
And well his looks command;
His features well his heart can mask,
With smiles and smoothness bland.

Gilbert has reasoned with his mind –
    He says 'twas all a dream;
He strives his inward sight to blind
    Against truth's inward beam.
He pitied not that shadowy thing,
    When it was flesh and blood;
Nor now can pity's balmy spring
    Refresh his arid mood.

'And if that dream has spoken truth,'
    Thus musingly he says;
'If Elinor be dead, in sooth,
    Such chance the shock repays:
A net was woven round my feet,
    I scarce could further go,
Ere Shame had forced a fast retreat,
    Dishonour brought me low.'

'Conceal her, then, deep, silent Sea,
    Give her a secret grave!
She sleeps in peace, and I am free,
    No longer Terror's slave:
And homage still, from all the world,
    Shall greet my spotless name,
Since surges break and waves are curled
    Above its threatened shame.'

III

THE WELCOME HOME

Above the city hangs the moon,
    Some clouds are boding rain;
Gilbert, erewhile on journey gone,
    Tonight comes home again.
Ten years have passed above his head,
    Each year has brought him gain;
His prosperous life has smoothly sped,
    Without or tear or stain.

'Tis somewhat late – the city clocks
    Twelve deep vibrations toll,
As Gilbert at the portal knocks,
    Which is his journey's goal.
The street is still and desolate,
    The moon hid by a cloud;
Gilbert, impatient, will not wait, –
    His second knock peals loud.

The clocks are hushed; there's not a light
    In any window nigh,
And not a single planet bright
    Looks from the clouded sky;
The air is raw, the rain descends,
    A bitter north-wind blows;
His cloak the traveller scarce defends –
    Will not the door unclose?

He knocks the third time, and the last;
    His summons now they hear,
Within, a footstep, hurrying fast,
    Is heard approaching near.
The bolt is drawn, the clanking chain
    Falls to the floor of stone;
And Gilbert to his heart will strain
    His wife and children soon.

The hand that lifts the latchet, holds
    A candle to his sight,
And Gilbert, on the step, beholds
    A woman, clad in white.
Lo! water from her dripping dress
    Runs on the streaming floor;
From every dark and clinging tress,
    The drops incessant pour.

There's none but her to welcome him;
    She holds the candle high,
And, motionless in form and limb,
    Stands cold and silent nigh;
There's sand and sea-weed on her robe,
    Her hollow eyes are blind;
No pulse in such a frame can throb,
    No life is there defined.

Gilbert turned ashy-white, but still
    His lips vouchsafed no cry;
He spurred his strength and master-will
    To pass the figure by, –
But, moving slow, it faced him straight,
    It would not flinch nor quail:
Then first did Gilbert's strength abate,
    His stony firmness fail.

He sank upon his knees and prayed;
    The shape stood rigid there;
He called aloud for human aid,
    No human aid was near.
An accent strange did thus repeat
    Heaven's stern but just decree:
'The measure thou to her didst mete,
    To thee shall measured be!'

Gilbert sprang from his bended knees,
    By the pale spectre pushed,
And, wild as one whom demons seize,
    Up the hall-staircase rushed;
Entered his chamber – near the bed
    Sheathed steel and fire-arms hung –
Impelled by maniac purpose dread,
    He chose those stores among.

Across his throat, a keen-edged knife
    With vigorous hand he drew;
The wound was wide – his outraged life
    Rushed rash and redly through.
And thus died, by a shameful death,
    A wise and worldly man,
Who never drew but selfish breath
    Since first his life began.

CURRER

The Prisoner

A FRAGMENT

In the dungeon-crypts, idly did I stray,
Reckless of the lives wasting there away;
'Draw the ponderous bars! open, Warder stern!'
He dared not say me nay – the hinges harshly turn.

'Our guests are darkly lodged,' I whisper'd, gazing
    through
The vault, whose grated eye showed heaven more grey
    than blue;
(This was when glad spring laughed in awaking pride;)
'Aye, darkly lodged enough!' returned my sullen guide.

Then, God forgive my youth; forgive my careless tongue;
I scoffed, as the chill chains on the damp flag-stones rung:
'Confined in triple walls, art thou so much to fear,
That we must bind thee down and clench thy fetters here?'

The captive raised her face, it was as soft and mild
As sculptured marble saint, or slumbering unwean'd
    child;
It was so soft and mild, it was so sweet and fair,
Pain could not trace a line, nor grief a shadow there!

The captive raised her hand and pressed it to her brow;
'I have been struck,' she said, 'and I am suffering now;
Yet these are little worth, your bolts and irons strong,
And, were they forged in steel, they could not hold me
    long.'

Hoarse laughed the jailor grim: 'Shall I be won to hear;
Dost think, fond, dreaming wretch, that *I* shall grant thy
    prayer?
Or, better still, wilt melt my master's heart with groans?
Ah! sooner might the sun thaw down these granite stones.

'My master's voice is low, his aspect bland and kind,
But hard as hardest flint, the soul that lurks behind;
And I am rough and rude, yet not more rough to see
Than is the hidden ghost that has its home in me.'

About her lips there played a smile of almost scorn,
'My friend,' she gently said, 'you have not heard me mourn;
When you my kindred's lives, *my* lost life, can restore,
Then may I weep and sue, – but never, friend, before!

Still, let my tyrants know, I am not doomed to wear
Year after year in gloom, and desolate despair;
A messenger of Hope, comes every night to me,
And offers for short life, eternal liberty.

He comes with western winds, with evening's wandering
        airs,
With that clear dusk of heaven that brings the thickest stars.
Winds take a pensive tone, and stars a tender fire,
And visions rise, and change, that kill me with desire.

Desire for nothing known in my maturer years,
When Joy grew mad with awe, at counting future tears.
When, if my spirit's sky was full of flashes warm,
I knew not whence they came, from sun, or thunder storm.

But, first, a hush of peace – a soundless calm descends;
The struggle of distress, and fierce impatience ends.
Mute music soothes my breast, unuttered harmony,
That I could never dream, till Earth was lost to me.

Then dawns the Invisible; the Unseen its truth reveals;
My outward sense is gone, my inward essence feels:
Its wings are almost free – its home, its harbour found,
Measuring the gulph, it stoops, and dares the final bound.

Oh, dreadful is the check – intense the agony –
When the ear begins to hear, and the eye begins to see;
When the pulse begins to throb, the brain to think again,
The soul to feel the flesh, and the flesh to feel the chain.

Yet I would lose no sting, would wish no torture less,
The more that anguish racks, the earlier it will bless;
And robed in fires of hell, or bright with heavenly shine,
If it but herald death, the vision is divine!'

She ceased to speak, and we, unanswering, turned to go –
We had no further power to work the captive woe:
Her cheek, her gleaming eye, declared that man had given
A sentence, unapproved, and overruled by Heaven.

ELLIS

If This be All

O God! if this indeed be all
    That Life can show to me;
If on my aching brow may fall
    No freshening dew from Thee, –

If with no brighter light than this
    The lamp of hope may glow,
And I may only *dream* of bliss,
    And wake to weary woe;

If friendship's solace must decay,
    When other joys are gone,
And love must keep so far away,
    While I go wandering on, –

Wandering and toiling without gain,
    The slave of others' will,
With constant care, and frequent pain,
    Despised, forgotten still;

Grieving to look on vice and sin,
    Yet powerless to quell
The silent current from within,
    The outward torrent's swell:

While all the good I would impart,
    The feelings I would share,
Are driven backward to my heart,
    And turned to wormwood, there;

If clouds must *ever* keep from sight
    The glories of the Sun,
And I must suffer Winter's blight,
    Ere Summer is begun;

If Life must be so full of care,
   Then call me soon to Thee;
Or give me strength enough to bear
   My load of misery.

ACTON

Life

Life, believe, is not a dream
   So dark as sages say;
Oft a little morning rain
   Foretells a pleasant day.
Sometimes there are clouds of gloom,
   But these are transient all;
If the shower will make the roses bloom,
   O why lament its fall?
     Rapidly, merrily,
   Life's sunny hours flit by,
     Gratefully, cheerily,
   Enjoy them as they fly!

What though Death at times steps in,
   And calls our Best away?
What though sorrow seems to win,
   O'er hope, a heavy sway?
Yet hope again elastic springs,
   Unconquered, though she fell;
Still buoyant are her golden wings,
   Still strong to bear us well.
     Manfully, fearlessly,
   The day of trial bear,
     For gloriously, victoriously,
   Can courage quell despair!

CURRER

Hope

Hope was but a timid friend;
   She sat without the grated den,
Watching how my fate would tend,
   Even as selfish-hearted men.

She was cruel in her fear;
   Through the bars, one dreary day,
I looked out to see her there,
   And she turned her face away!

Like a false guard, false watch keeping,
   Still, in strife, she whispered peace;
She would sing while I was weeping;
   If I listened, she would cease.

False she was, and unrelenting;
   When my last joys strewed the ground,
Even Sorrow saw, repenting,
   Those sad relics scattered round;

Hope, whose whisper would have given
   Balm to all my frenzied pain,
Stretched her wings, and soared to heaven,
   Went, and ne'er returned again!

ELLIS

Memory

Brightly the sun of summer shone,
Green fields and waving woods upon,
   And soft winds wandered by;
Above, a sky of purest blue,
Around, bright flowers of loveliest hue,
   Allured the gazer's eye.

But what were all these charms to me,
When one sweet breath of memory
   Came gently wafting by?
I closed my eyes against the day,
And called my willing soul away,
   From earth, and air, and sky;

That I might simply fancy there
One little flower – a primrose fair,
   Just opening into sight;
As in the days of infancy,
An opening primrose seemed to me
   A source of strange delight.

Sweet Memory! ever smile on me;
Nature's chief beauties spring from thee;
   Oh, still thy tribute bring!
Still make the golden crocus shine
Among the flowers the most divine,
   The glory of the spring.

Still in the wall-flower's fragrance dwell;
And hover round the slight blue bell,
   My childhood's darling flower.
Smile on the little daisy still,
The buttercup's bright goblet fill
   With all thy former power.

For ever hang thy dreamy spell
Round mountain star and heather bell,
   And do not pass away
From sparkling frost, or wreathed snow,
And whisper when the wild winds blow,
   Or rippling waters play.

Is childhood, then, so all divine?
Or Memory, is the glory thine,
   That haloes thus the past?
Not *all* divine; its pangs of grief,
(Although, perchance, their stay be brief,)
   Are bitter while they last.

Nor is the glory all thine own,
For on our earliest joys alone
   That holy light is cast.
With such a ray, no spell of thine
Can make our later pleasures shine,
   Though long ago they passed.

ACTON

The Letter

What is she writing? Watch her now,
    How fast her fingers move!
How eagerly her youthful brow
    Is bent in thought above!
Her long curls, drooping, shade the light,
    She puts them quick aside,
Nor knows, that band of crystals bright,
    Her hasty touch untied.
It slips adown her silken dress,
    Falls glittering at her feet;
Unmarked it falls, for she no less
    Pursues her labour sweet.

The very loveliest hour that shines,
    Is in that deep blue sky;
The golden sun of June declines,
    It has not caught her eye.
The cheerful lawn, and unclosed gate,
    The white road, far away,
In vain for her light footsteps wait,
    She comes not forth today.
There is an open door of glass
    Close by that lady's chair,
From thence, to slopes of mossy grass,
    Descends a marble stair.

Tall plants of bright and spicy bloom
    Around the threshold grow;
Their leaves and blossoms shade the room,
    From that sun's deepening glow.
Why does she not a moment glance
    Between the clustering flowers,
And mark in heaven the radiant dance
    Of evening's rosy hours?
O look again! Still fixed her eye,

Unsmiling, earnest, still,
And fast her pen and fingers fly,
   Urged by her eager will.

Her soul is in th' absorbing task;
   To whom, then, doth she write?
Nay, watch her still more closely, ask
   Her own eyes' serious light;
Where do they turn, as now her pen
   Hangs o'er th' unfinished line?
Whence fell the tearful gleam that then
   Did in their dark spheres shine?
The summer-parlour looks so dark,
   When from that sky you turn,
And from th' expanse of that green park,
   You scarce may aught discern.

Yet o'er the piles of porcelain rare,
   O'er flower-stand, couch, and vase,
Sloped, as if leaning on the air,
   One picture meets the gaze.
'Tis there she turns; you may not see
   Distinct, what form defines
The clouded mass of mystery
   Yon broad gold frame confines.
But look again; inured to shade
   Your eyes now faintly trace
A stalwart form, a massive head,
   A firm, determined face.

Black Spanish locks, a sunburnt cheek,
   A brow high, broad, and white,
Where every furrow seems to speak
   Of mind and moral might.
Is that her god? I cannot tell;
   Her eye a moment met
Th' impending picture, then it fell
   Darkened and dimmed and wet.
A moment more, her task is done,

And sealed the letter lies;
And now, towards the setting sun
    She turns her tearful eyes.

Those tears flow over, wonder not,
    For by the inscription, see
In what a strange and distant spot
    Her heart of hearts must be!
Three seas and many a league of land
    That letter must pass o'er,
E'er read by him to whose loved hand
    'Tis sent from England's shore.

Remote colonial wilds detain
Her husband, loved though stern;
She, 'mid that smiling English scene,
Weeps for his wished return.

CURRER

A Day Dream

On a sunny brae, alone I lay
    One summer afternoon;
It was the marriage-time of May
    With her young lover, June.

From her mother's heart, seemed loath to part
    That queen of bridal charms,
But her father smiled on the fairest child
    He ever held in his arms.

The trees did wave their plumy crests,
    The glad birds caroled clear;
And I, of all the wedding guests,
    Was only sullen there!

There was not one, but wished to shun
    My aspect void of cheer;
The very grey rocks, looking on,
    Asked, 'What do you do here?'

And I could utter no reply;
    In sooth, I did not know
Why I had brought a clouded eye
    To greet the general glow.

So, resting on a heathy bank,
    I took my heart to me;
And we together sadly sank
    Into a reverie.

We thought, 'When winter comes again,
    Where will these bright things be?
All vanished, like a vision vain,
    An unreal mockery!

The birds that now so blithely sing,
   Through deserts, frozen dry,
Poor spectres of the perished spring,
   In famished troops, will fly.

And why should we be glad at all?
   The leaf is hardly green,
Before a token of its fall
   Is on the surface seen!'

Now, whether it were really so,
   I never could be sure;
But as in fit of peevish woe,
   I stretched me on the moor.

A thousand thousand gleaming fires
   Seemed kindling in the air;
A thousand thousand silvery lyres
   Resounded far and near:

Methought, the very breath I breathed
   Was full of sparks divine,
And all my heather couch was wreathed
   By that celestial shine!

And, while the wide earth echoing rung
   To their strange minstrelsy,
The little glittering spirits sung,
   Or seemed to sing, to me.

'O mortal! mortal! let them die;
   Let time and tears destroy,
That we may overflow the sky
   With universal joy!

Let grief distract the sufferer's breast,
   And night obscure his way;
They hasten him to endless rest,
   And everlasting day.

To thee the world is like a tomb,
   A desert's naked shore;
To us, in unimagined bloom,
   It brightens more and more!

And, could we lift the veil, and give
   One brief glimpse to thine eye,
Thou wouldst rejoice for those that live,
   Because they live to die.'

The music ceased; the noonday dream,
   Like dream of night, withdrew;
But Fancy, still, will sometimes deem
   Her fond creation true.

ELLIS

To Cowper

Sweet are thy strains, celestial Bard;
    And oft, in childhood's years,
I've read them o'er and o'er again,
    With floods of silent tears.

The language of my inmost heart,
    I traced in every line;
My sins, *my* sorrows, hopes, and fears,
    Were there – and only mine.

All for myself the sigh would swell,
    The tear of anguish start;
I little knew what wilder woe
    Had filled the Poet's heart.

I did not know the nights of gloom,
    The days of misery;
The long, long years of dark despair,
    That crushed and tortured thee.

But, they are gone; from earth at length
    Thy gentle soul is pass'd,
And in the bosom of its God
    Has found its home at last.

It must be so, if God is love,
    And answers fervent prayer;
Then surely thou shalt dwell on high,
    And I may meet thee there.

Is he the source of every good,
    The spring of purity?
Then in thine hours of deepest woe,
    Thy God was still with thee.

How else, when every hope was fled,
   Couldst thou so fondly cling
To holy things and holy men?
   And how so sweetly sing,

Of things that God alone could teach?
   And whence that purity,
That hatred of all sinful ways –
   That gentle charity?

Are *these* the symptoms of a heart
   Of heavenly grace bereft:
For ever banished from its God,
   To Satan's fury left?

Yet, should thy darkest fears be true,
   If Heaven be so severe,
That such a soul as thine is lost, –
   Oh! how shall *I* appear?

ACTON

Regret

Long ago I wished to leave
'The house where I was born;'
Long ago I used to grieve,
My home seemed so forlorn.
In other years, its silent rooms
Were filled with haunting fears;
Now, their very memory comes
O'ercharged with tender tears.

Life and marriage I have known,
Things once deemed so bright;
Now, how utterly is flown
Every ray of light!
'Mid the unknown sea of life
I no blest isle have found;
At last, through all its wild wave's strife,
My bark is homeward bound.

Farewell, dark and rolling deep!
Farewell, foreign shore!
Open, in unclouded sweep,
Thou glorious realm before!
Yet, though I had safely pass'd
That weary, vexed main,
One loved voice, through surge and blast,
Could call me back again.

Though the soul's bright morning rose
O'er Paradise for me,
William! even from Heaven's repose
I'd turn, invoked by thee!
Storm nor surge should e'er arrest
My soul, exulting then:
All my heaven was once thy breast,
Would it were mine again!

CURRER

To Imagination

When weary with the long day's care,
   And earthly change from pain to pain,
And lost and ready to despair,
   Thy kind voice calls me back again:
Oh, my true friend! I am not lone,
While thou canst speak with such a tone!

So hopeless is the world without;
   The world within I doubly prize;
Thy world, where guile, and hate, and doubt,
   And cold suspicion never rise;
Where thou, and I, and Liberty,
Have undisputed sovereignty.

What matters it, that, all around,
   Danger, and guilt, and darkness lie,
If but within our bosom's bound
   We hold a bright, untroubled sky.
Warm with ten thousand mingled rays
Of suns that know no winter days?

Reason, indeed, may oft complain
   For Nature's sad reality,
And tell the suffering heart, how vain
   Its cherished dreams must always be;
And Truth may rudely trample down
The flowers of Fancy, newly-blown:

But, thou art ever there, to bring
   The hovering vision back, and breathe
New glories o'er the blighted spring,
   And call a lovelier Life from Death,
And whisper, with a voice divine,
Of real worlds, as bright as thine.

I trust not to thy phantom bliss,
    Yet, still, in evening's quiet hour,
With never-failing thankfulness,
    I welcome thee, Benignant Power;
Sure solacer of human cares,
And sweeter hope, when hope despairs!

ELLIS

The Doubter's Prayer

Eternal Power, of earth and air!
Unseen, yet seen in all around,
Remote, but dwelling everywhere,
Though silent, heard in every sound.

If e'er thine ear in mercy bent,
When wretched mortals cried to Thee,
And if, indeed, Thy Son was sent,
To save lost sinners such as me:

Then hear me now, while, kneeling here,
I lift to thee my heart and eye,
And all my soul ascends in prayer,
Oh, give me – give me Faith! I cry.

Without some glimmering in my heart,
I could not raise this fervent prayer;
But, oh! a stronger light impart,
And in Thy mercy fix it there.

While Faith is with me, I am blest;
It turns my darkest night to day;
But while I clasp it to my breast,
I often feel it slide away.

Then, cold and dark, my spirit sinks,
To see my light of life depart;
And every fiend of Hell, methinks,
Enjoys the anguish of my heart.

What shall I do, if all my love,
My hopes, my toil, are cast away,
And if there be no God above,
To hear and bless me when I pray?

If this be vain delusion all,
If death be an eternal sleep,
And none can hear my secret call,
Or see the silent tears I weep!

Oh, help me, God! For thou alone
Canst my distracted soul relieve;
Forsake it not: it is thine own,
Though weak, yet longing to believe.

Oh, drive these cruel doubts away;
And make me know, that Thou art God!
A faith, that shines by night and day,
Will lighten every earthly load.

If I believe that Jesus died,
And, waking, rose to reign above;
Then surely Sorrow, Sin, and Pride,
Must yield to Peace, and Hope, and Love.

And all the blessed words He said
Will strength and holy joy impart:
A shield of safety o'er my head,
A spring of comfort in my heart.

ACTON

Presentiment

'Sister, you've sat there all the day,
   Come to the hearth awhile;
The wind so wildly sweeps away,
   The clouds, so darkly pile.
That open book has lain, unread,
   For hours upon your knee;
You've never smiled nor turned your head
   What can you, sister, see?'

'Come hither, Jane, look down the field;
   How dense a mist creeps on!
The path, the hedge, are both concealed,
   Ev'n the white gate is gone;
No landscape through the fog I trace,
   No hill with pastures green;
All featureless is nature's face,
   All masked in clouds her mien.

'Scarce is the rustle of a leaf
   Heard in our garden now;
The year grows old, its days wax brief,
   The tresses leave its brow.
The rain drives fast before the wind,
   The sky is blank and grey;
O Jane, what sadness fills the mind
   On such a dreary day!'

'You think too much, my sister dear;
   You sit too long alone;
What though November days be drear?
   Full soon will they be gone.
I've swept the hearth, and placed your chair,
   Come, Emma, sit by me;
Our own fireside is never drear,
Though late and wintry wane the year,
   Though rough the night may be.'

'The peaceful glow of our fireside
   Imparts no peace to me:
My thoughts would rather wander wide
   Than rest, dear Jane, with thee.
I'm on a distant journey bound,
   And if, about my heart,
Too closely kindred ties were wound,
   'T would break when forced to part.

' "Soon will November days be o'er:"
   Well have you spoken, Jane:
My own forebodings tell me more,
For me, I know by presage sure,
   They'll ne'er return again.
Ere long, nor sun nor storm to me
   Will bring or joy or gloom;
They reach not that Eternity
   Which soon will be my home.'

Eight months are gone, the summer sun
   Sets in a glorious sky;
A quiet field, all green and lone,
   Receives its rosy dye.
Jane sits upon a shaded stile,
   Alone she sits there now;
Her head rests on her hand the while,
   And thought o'ercasts her brow.

She's thinking of one winter's day,
   A few short months ago,
When Emma's bier was borne away
   O'er wastes of frozen snow.
She's thinking how that drifted snow
   Dissolved in spring's first gleam,
And how her sister's memory now
   Fades, even as fades a dream.

The snow will whiten earth again,
  But Emma comes no more;
She left, 'mid winter's sleet and rain,
  This world for Heaven's far shore.
On Beulah's hills she wanders now,
  On Eden's tranquil plain;
To her shall Jane hereafter go,
  She ne'er shall come to Jane!

CURRER

How Clear She Shines

How clear she shines! How quietly
    I lie beneath her guardian light;
While heaven and earth are whispering me,
    'Tomorrow, wake, but, dream tonight.'
Yes, Fancy, come, my Fairy love!
    These throbbing temples softly kiss;
And bend my lonely couch above
    And bring me rest, and bring me bliss.

The world is going; dark world, adieu!
    Grim world, conceal thee till the day;
The heart, thou canst not all subdue,
    Must still resist, if thou delay!

Thy love I will not, will not share;
    Thy hatred only wakes a smile;
Thy griefs may wound – thy wrongs may tear,
    But, oh, thy lies shall ne'er beguile!
While gazing on the stars that glow
    Above me, in that stormless sea,
I long to hope that all the woe
    Creation knows, is held in thee!

And, this shall be my dream tonight;
    I'll think the heaven of glorious spheres
Is rolling on its course of light
    In endless bliss, through endless years;
I'll think, there's not one world above,
    Far as these straining eyes can see,
Where Wisdom ever laughed at Love,
    Or Virtue crouched to Infamy;

Where, writhing 'neath the strokes of Fate,
  The mangled wretch was forced to smile;
To match his patience 'gainst her hate,
  His heart rebellious all the while.
Where Pleasure still will lead to wrong,
  And helpless Reason warn in vain;
And Truth is weak, and Treachery strong;
  And Joy the surest path to Pain;
And Peace, the lethargy of Grief;
  And Hope, a phantom of the soul;
And Life, a labour, void and brief;
  And Death, the despot of the whole!

ELLIS

A Word to the 'Elect'

You may rejoice to think *yourselves* secure;
You may be grateful for the gift divine –
That grace unsought, which made your black hearts pure,
And fits your earth-born souls in Heaven to shine.

But, is it sweet to look around, and view
Thousands excluded from that happiness
Which they deserved, at least, as much as you, –
Their faults not greater, nor their virtues less?

And, wherefore should you love your God the more,
Because to you alone his smiles are given;
Because he chose to pass the *many* o'er,
And only bring the favoured *few* to Heaven?

And, wherefore should your hearts more grateful prove,
Because for ALL the Saviour did not die?
Is yours the God of justice and of love?
And are your bosoms warm with charity?

Say, does your heart expand to all mankind?
And, would you ever to your neighbour do –
The weak, the strong, the enlightened, and the blind –
As you would have your neighbour do to you?

And, when you, looking on your fellow-men,
Behold them doomed to endless misery,
How can you talk of joy and rapture then? –
May God withhold such cruel joy from me!

That none deserve eternal bliss I know;
Unmerited the grace in mercy given:
But, none shall sink to everlasting woe,
That have not well deserved the wrath of Heaven.

And, oh! there lives within my heart
   A hope, long nursed by me;
(And, should its cheering ray depart,
   How dark my soul would be!)

That as in Adam all have died,
   In Christ shall all men live;
And ever round his throne abide,
   Eternal praise to give.

That even the wicked shall at last
   Be fitted for the skies;
And, when their dreadful doom is past,
   To life and light arise.

I ask not, how remote the day,
   Nor what the sinners' woe,
Before their dross is purged away;
   Enough for me, to know

That when the cup of wrath is drained,
   The metal purified,
They'll cling to what they once disdained,
   And live by Him that died.

ACTON

The Teacher's Monologue

The room is quiet, thoughts alone
People its mute tranquillity;
The yoke put off, the long task done, –
I am, as it is bliss to be,
Still and untroubled. Now, I see,
For the first time, how soft the day
O'er waveless water, stirless tree,
Silent and sunny, wings its way.
Now, as I watch that distant hill,
So faint, so blue, so far removed,
Sweet dreams of home my heart may fill,
That home where I am known and loved:
It lies beyond; yon azure brow
Parts me from all Earth holds for me;
And, morn and eve, my yearnings flow
Thitherward tending, changelessly.
My happiest hours, aye! all the time,
I love to keep in memory,
Lapsed among moors, ere life's first prime
Decayed to dark anxiety.

Sometimes, I think a narrow heart
Makes me thus mourn those far away,
And keeps my love so far apart
From friends and friendships of today;
Sometimes, I think 'tis but a dream
I treasure up so jealously,
All the sweet thoughts I live on seem
To vanish into vacancy:
And then, this strange, coarse world around
Seems all that's palpable and true;
And every sight, and every sound,
Combines my spirit to subdue
To aching grief, so void and lone
Is Life and Earth – so worse than vain,

The hopes that, in my own heart sown,
And cherished by such sun and rain
As Joy and transient Sorrow shed,
Have ripened to a harvest there:
Alas! methinks I hear it said,
'Thy golden sheaves are empty air.'

All fades away; my very home
I think will soon be desolate;
I hear, at times, a warning come
Of bitter partings at its gate;
And, if I should return and see
The hearth-fire quenched, the vacant chair;
And hear it whispered mournfully,
That farewells have been spoken there,
What shall I do, and whither turn?
Where look for peace? When cease to mourn?

*　*　*

'Tis not the air I wished to play,
　The strain I wished to sing;
My wilful spirit slipped away
　And struck another string.
I neither wanted smile nor tear,
　Bright joy nor bitter woe,
But just a song that sweet and clear,
　Though haply sad, might flow.

A quiet song, to solace me
　When sleep refused to come;
A strain to chase despondency,
　When sorrowful for home.
In vain I try; I cannot sing;
　All feels so cold and dead;
No wild distress, no gushing spring
　Of tears in anguish shed;

But all the impatient gloom of one
    Who waits a distant day,
When, some great task of suffering done,
    Repose shall toil repay.
For youth departs, and pleasure flies,
    And life consumes away,
And youth's rejoicing ardour dies
    Beneath this drear delay;

And Patience, weary with her yoke,
    Is yielding to despair,
And Health's elastic spring is broke
    Beneath the strain of care.
Life will be gone ere I have lived;
    Where now is Life's first prime?
I've worked and studied, longed and grieved,
    Through all that rosy time.

To toil, to think, to long, to grieve, –
    Is such my future fate?
The morn was dreary, must the eve
    Be also desolate?
Well, such a life at least makes Death
    A welcome, wished-for friend;
Then, aid me, Reason, Patience, Faith,
    To suffer to the end!

CURRER

Sympathy

There should be no despair for you
   While nightly stars are burning;
While evening pours its silent dew
   And sunshine gilds the morning.
There should be no despair – though tears
   May flow down like a river:
Are not the best beloved of years
   Around your heart for ever?

They weep, you weep, it must be so;
   Winds sigh as you are sighing,
And Winter sheds his grief in snow
   Where Autumn's leaves are lying:
Yet, these revive, and from their fate
   Your fate cannot be parted:
Then, journey on, if not elate,
   Still, *never* broken-hearted!

ELLIS

Past Days

'Tis strange to think, there *was* a time
When mirth was not an empty name,
When laughter really cheered the heart,
And frequent smiles unbidden came,
And tears of grief would only flow
In sympathy for others' woe;

When speech expressed the inward thought,
And heart to kindred heart was bare,
And Summer days were far too short
For all the pleasures crowded there,
And silence, solitude, and rest,
Now welcome to the weary breast –

Were all unprized, uncourted then –
And all the joy one spirit showed,
The other deeply felt again;
And friendship like a river flowed,
Constant and strong its silent course,
For nought withstood its gentle force:

When night, the holy time of peace,
Was dreaded as the parting hour;
When speech and mirth at once must cease,
And Silence must resume her power;
Though ever free from pains and woes,
She only brought us calm repose.

And when the blessed dawn again
Brought daylight to the blushing skies,
We woke, and not *reluctant* then,
To joyless *labour* did we rise;
But full of hope, and glad and gay,
We welcomed the returning day.

ACTON

Passion

Some have won a wild delight,
  By daring wilder sorrow;
Could I gain thy love tonight,
  I'd hazard death tomorrow.

Could the battle-struggle earn
  One kind glance from thine eye,
How this withering heart would burn,
  The heady fight to try!

Welcome nights of broken sleep,
  And days of carnage cold,
Could I deem that thou wouldst weep
  To hear my perils told.

Tell me, if with wandering bands
  I roam full far away,
Wilt thou, to those distant lands,
  In spirit ever stray?

Wild, long, a trumpet sounds afar;
  Bid me – bid me go
Where Seik and Briton meet in war,
  On Indian Sutlej's flow.

Blood has dyed the Sutlej's waves
  With scarlet stain, I know;
Indus' borders yawn with graves,
  Yet, command me go!

Though rank and high the holocaust
  Of nations, steams to heaven,
Glad I'd join the death-doomed host,
  Were but the mandate given.

Passion's strength should nerve my arm,
    Its ardour stir my life,
Till human force to that dread charm
    Should yield and sink in wild alarm,
Like trees to tempest-strife.

If, hot from war, I seek thy love,
    Darest thou turn aside?
Darest thou, then, my fire reprove,
    By scorn, and maddening pride?

No – my will shall yet control
    Thy will, so high and free,
And love shall tame that haughty soul –
    Yes – tenderest love for me.

I'll read my triumph in thine eyes,
    Behold, and prove the change;
Then leave, perchance, my noble prize,
    Once more in arms to range.

I'd die when all the foam is up,
    The bright wine sparkling high;
Nor wait till in the exhausted cup
    Life's dull dregs only lie.

Then Love thus crowned with sweet reward,
    Hope blest with fulness large,
I'd mount the saddle, draw the sword,
    And perish in the charge!

CURRER

Preference

Not in scorn do I reprove thee,
Not in pride thy vows I waive,
But, believe, I could not love thee,
Wert thou prince, and I a slave.
These, then, are thine oaths of passion?
This, thy tenderness for me?
Judged, even, by thine own confession,
Thou art steeped in perfidy.
Having vanquished, thou wouldst leave me!
Thus I read thee long ago;
Therefore, dared I not deceive thee,
Even with friendship's gentle show.
Therefore, with impassive coldness
Have I ever met thy gaze;
Though, full oft, with daring boldness,
Thou thine eyes to mine didst raise.
Why that smile? Thou now art deeming
This my coldness all untrue, –
But a mask of frozen seeming,
Hiding secret fires from view.
Touch my hand, thou self-deceiver;
Nay – be calm, for I am so:
Does it burn? Does my lip quiver?
Has mine eye a troubled glow?
Canst thou call a moment's colour
To my forehead – to my cheek?
Canst thou tinge their tranquil pallor
With one flattering, feverish streak?
Am I marble? What! no woman
Could so calm before thee stand?
Nothing living, sentient, human,
Could so coldly take thy hand?
Yes – a sister might, a mother:
My good-will is sisterly:
Dream not, then, I strive to smother

Fires that inly burn for thee.
Rave not, rage not, wrath is fruitless,
Fury cannot change my mind;
I but deem the feeling rootless
Which so whirls in passion's wind.
Can I love? Oh, deeply – truly –
Warmly – fondly – but not thee;
And my love is answered duly,
With an equal energy.
Wouldst thou see thy rival? Hasten,
Draw that curtain soft aside,
Look where yon thick branches chasten
Noon, with shades of eventide.
In that glade, where foliage blending
Forms a green arch overhead,
Sits thy rival thoughtful bending
O'er a stand with papers spread –
Motionless, his fingers plying
That untired, unresting pen;
Time and tide unnoticed flying,
There he sits – the first of men!
Man of conscience – man of reason;
Stern, perchance, but ever just;
Foe to falsehood, wrong, and treason,
Honour's shield, and virtue's trust!
Worker, thinker, firm defender
Of Heaven's truth – man's liberty;
Soul of iron – proof to slander,
Rock where founders tyranny.
Fame he seeks not – but full surely
She will seek him, in his home;
This I know, and wait securely
For the atoning hour to come.
To that man my faith is given,
Therefore, soldier, cease to sue;
While God reigns in earth and heaven,
I to him will still be true!

CURRER

Plead for Me

Oh, thy bright eyes must answer now,
When Reason, with a scornful brow,
Is mocking at my overthrow!
Oh, thy sweet tongue must plead for me
And tell, why I have chosen thee!

Stern Reason is to judgment come,
Arrayed in all her forms of gloom:
Wilt thou, my advocate, be dumb?
No, radiant angel, speak and say,
Why I did cast the world away.

Why I have persevered to shun
The common paths that others run,
And on a strange road journeyed on,
Heedless, alike, of wealth and power –
Of glory's wreath and pleasure's flower.

These, once, indeed, seemed Beings Divine;
And they, perchance, heard vows of mine,
And saw my offerings on their shrine;
But, careless gifts are seldom prized,
And *mine* were worthily despised.

So, with a ready heart I swore
To seek their altar-stone no more;
And gave my spirit to adore
Thee, ever-present, phantom thing;
My slave, my comrade, and my king,

A slave, because I rule thee still;
Incline thee to my changeful will,
And make thy influence good or ill:
A comrade, for by day and night
Thou art my intimate delight, –

My darling pain that wounds and sears
And wrings a blessing out from tears
By deadening me to earthly cares;
And yet, a king, though Prudence well
Have taught thy subject to rebel.

And am I wrong to worship, where
Faith cannot doubt, nor hope despair,
Since my own soul can grant my prayer?
Speak, God of visions, plead for me,
And tell why I have chosen thee!

ELLIS

The Consolation

Though bleak these woods, and
    damp the ground
With fallen leaves so thickly strown,
And cold the wind that wanders round
With wild and melancholy moan;

There is a friendly roof, I know,
Might shield me from the wintry blast;
There is a fire, whose ruddy glow
Will cheer me for my wanderings past.

And so, though still, where'er I go,
Cold stranger-glances meet my eye;
Though, when my spirit sinks in woe,
Unheeded swells the unbidden sigh;

Though solitude, endured too long,
Bids youthful joys too soon decay,
Makes mirth a stranger to my tongue,
And overclouds my noon of day;

When kindly thoughts, that would have way,
Flow back discouraged to my breast; –
I know there is, though far away,
A home where heart and soul may rest.

Warm hands are there, that, clasped in mine,
The warmer heart will not belie;
While mirth, and truth, and friendship shine
In smiling lip and earnest eye.

The ice that gathers round my heart
May there be thawed; and sweetly, then,
The joys of youth, that now depart,
Will come to cheer my soul again.

Though far I roam, that thought shall be
My hope, my comfort, everywhere;
While such a home remains to me,
My heart shall never know despair!

ACTON

Evening Solace

The human heart has hidden treasures,
In secret kept, in silence sealed; –
The thoughts, the hopes, the dreams, the pleasures,
Whose charms were broken if revealed.
And days may pass in gay confusion,
And nights in rosy riot fly,
While, lost in Fame's or Wealth's illusion,
The memory of the Past may die.

But, there are hours of lonely musing,
Such as in evening silence come,
When, soft as birds their pinions closing,
The heart's best feelings gather home.
Then in our souls there seems to languish
A tender grief that is not woe;
And thoughts that once wrung groans of anguish,
Now cause but some mild tears to flow.

And feelings, once as strong as passions,
Float softly back – a faded dream;
Our own sharp griefs and wild sensations,
The tale of others' sufferings seem.
Oh! when the heart is freshly bleeding,
How longs it for that time to be,
When, through the mist of years receding,
Its woes but live in reverie!

And it can dwell on moonlight glimmer,
On evening shade and loneliness;
And, while the sky grows dim and dimmer,
Feel no untold and strange distress –
Only a deeper impulse given
By lonely hour and darkened room,
To solemn thoughts that soar to heaven,
Seeking a life and world to come.

CURRER

Self-Interrogation

'The evening passes fast away,
   'Tis almost time to rest;
What thoughts has left the vanished day,
   What feelings, in thy breast?

'The vanished day? It leaves a sense
   Of labour hardly done;
Of little, gained with vast expense, –
   A sense of grief alone!

'Time stands before the door of Death,
   Upbraiding bitterly;
And Conscience, with exhaustless breath,
   Pours black reproach on me:

'And though I've said that Conscience lies,
   And Time should Fate condemn;
Still, sad Repentance clouds my eyes,
   And makes me yield to them!

'Then art thou glad to seek repose?
   Art glad to leave the sea,
And anchor all thy weary woes
   In calm Eternity?

'Nothing regrets to see thee go –
   Not one voice sobs "farewell,"
And where thy heart has suffered so,
   Canst thou desire to dwell?'

'Alas! The countless links are strong
   That bind us to our clay;
The loving spirit lingers long,
   And would not pass away!

'And rest is sweet, when laurelled fame
    Will crown the soldier's crest;
But, a brave heart, with a tarnished name,
    Would rather fight than rest.'

'Well, thou hast fought for many a year,
    Hast fought thy whole life through,
Hast humbled Falsehood, trampled Fear;
    What is there left to do?'

' 'Tis true, this arm has hotly striven,
    Has dared what few would dare;
Much have I done, and freely given,
    But little learnt to bear!'

'Look on the grave, where thou must sleep,
    Thy last, and strongest foe;
It is endurance not to weep,
    If that repose seem woe.

'The long war closing in defeat,
    Defeat serenely borne,
Thy midnight rest may still be sweet,
    And break in glorious morn!'

ELLIS

Lines Composed in a Wood on a Windy Day

My soul is awakened, my spirit is soaring
And carried aloft on the wings of the breeze;
For above and around me the wild wind is roaring,
Arousing to rapture the earth and the seas.

The long withered grass in the sunshine is glancing,
The bare trees are tossing their branches on high;
The dead leaves, beneath them, are merrily dancing,
The white clouds are scudding across the blue sky.

I wish I could see how the ocean is lashing
The foam of its billows to whirlwinds of spray;
I wish I could see how its proud waves are dashing,
And hear the wild roar of their thunder today!

ACTON

Stanzas

If thou be in a lonely place,
　If one hour's calm be thine,
As Evening bends her placid face
　O'er this sweet day's decline;
If all the earth and all the heaven
　Now look serene to thee,
As o'er them shuts the summer even,
　One moment – think of me!

Pause, in the lane, returning home;
　'Tis dusk, it will be still:
Pause near the elm, a sacred gloom
　Its breezeless boughs will fill.
Look at that soft and golden light,
　High in the unclouded sky;
Watch the last bird's belated flight,
　As it flits silent by.

Hark! for a sound upon the wind,
　A step, a voice, a sigh;
If all be still, then yield thy mind,
　Unchecked, to memory.
If thy love were like mine, how blest
　That twilight hour would seem,
When, back from the regretted Past,
　Returned our early dream!

If thy love were like mine, how wild
　Thy longings, even to pain,
For sunset soft, and moonlight mild,
　To bring that hour again!
But oft, when in thine arms I lay,
　I've seen thy dark eyes shine,
And deeply felt, their changeful ray
　Spoke other love than mine.

My love is almost anguish now,
　　It beats so strong and true;
'Twere rapture, could I deem that thou
Such anguish ever knew.
I have been but thy transient flower,
　　Thou wert my god divine;
Till, checked by death's congealing power,
　　This heart must throb for thine.

And well my dying hour were blest,
　　If life's expiring breath
Should pass, as thy lips gently prest
　　My forehead, cold in death;
And sound my sleep would be, and sweet,
　　Beneath the churchyard tree,
If sometimes in thy heart should beat
　　One pulse, still true to me.

CURRER

Death

Death! that struck when I was most confiding
In my certain faith of joy to be —
Strike again, Time's withered branch dividing
From the fresh root of Eternity!

Leaves, upon Time's branch, were growing brightly,
Full of sap, and full of silver dew;
Birds beneath its shelter gathered nightly;
Daily round its flowers the wild bees flew.

Sorrow passed, and plucked the golden blossom;
Guilt stripped off the foliage in its pride;
Bit, within its parent's kindly bosom,
Flowed for ever Life's restoring tide.

Little mourned I for the parted gladness,
For the vacant nest and silent song –
Hope was there, and laughed me out of sadness;
Whispering, 'Winter will not linger long!'

And, behold! with tenfold increase blessing,
Spring adorned the beauty-burdened spray;
Wind and rain and fervent heat, caressing,
Lavished glory on that second May!

High it rose – no winged grief could sweep it;
Sin was scared to distance with its shine;
Love, and its own life, had power to keep it
From all wrong – from every blight but thine!

Cruel Death! The young leaves droop and languish;
Evening's gentle air may still restore –
No! the morning sunshine mocks my anguish –
Time, for me, must never blossom more!

Strike it down, that other boughs may flourish
Where that perished sapling used to be;
Thus, at least, its mouldering corpse will nourish
That from which it sprung – Eternity.

ELLIS

Views of Life

When sinks my heart in hopeless gloom,
And life can show no joy for me;
And I behold a yawning tomb,
Where bowers and palaces should be;

In vain you talk of morbid dreams;
In vain you gaily smiling say,
That what to me so dreary seems,
The healthy mind deems bright and gay.

I too have smiled, and thought like you,
But madly smiled, and falsely deemed:
Truth led me to the present view,
I'm waking now – 'twas *then* I dreamed.

I lately saw a sunset sky,
And stood enraptured to behold
Its varied hues of glorious dye:
First, fleecy clouds of shining gold;

These blushing took a rosy hue;
Beneath them shone a flood of green;
Nor less divine, the glorious blue
That smiled above them and between.

I cannot name each lovely shade;
I cannot say how bright they shone;
But one by one, I saw them fade;
And what remained when they were gone?

Dull clouds remained, of sombre hue,
And when their borrowed charm was o'er,
The azure sky had faded too,
That smiled so softly bright before.

So, gilded by the glow of youth,
Our varied life looks fair and gay;
And so remains the naked truth,
When that false light is past away.

Why blame ye, then, my keener sight,
That clearly sees a world of woes,
Through all the haze of golden light,
That flattering Falsehood round it throws?

When the young mother smiles above
The first-born darling of her heart,
Her bosom glows with earnest love,
While tears of silent transport start.

Fond dreamer! little does she know
The anxious toil, the suffering,
The blasted hopes, the burning woe,
The object of her joy will bring.

Her blinded eyes behold not now
What, soon or late, must be his doom;
The anguish that will cloud his brow,
The bed of death, the dreary tomb.

As little know the youthful pair,
In mutual love supremely blest,
What weariness, and cold despair,
Ere long, will seize the aching breast.

And, even, should Love and Faith remain,
(The greatest blessings life can show,)
Amid adversity and pain,
To shine, throughout with cheering glow;

They do not see how cruel Death
Comes on, their loving hearts to part:
One feels not now the gasping breath,
The rending of the earth-bound heart, –

The soul's and body's agony,
Ere she may sink to her repose.
The sad survivor cannot see
The grave above his darling close;

Nor how, despairing and alone,
He then must wear his life away;
And linger, feebly toiling on,
And fainting, sink into decay.

* * *

Oh, Youth may listen patiently,
While sad Experience tells her tale;
But Doubt sits smiling in his eye,
For ardent Hope will still prevail!

He hears how feeble Pleasure dies,
By guilt destroyed, and pain and woe;
He turns to Hope – and she replies,
'Believe it not – it is not so!'

'Oh, heed her not!' Experience says,
'For thus she whispered once to me;
She told me, in my youthful days,
How glorious manhood's prime would be.

When, in the time of early Spring,
Too chill the winds that o'er me pass'd,
She said, each coming day would bring
A fairer heaven, a gentler blast.

And when the sun too seldom beamed,
The sky, o'ercast, too darkly frowned,
The soaking rain too constant streamed,
And mists too dreary gathered round;

She told me, Summer's glorious ray
Would chase those vapours all away,
    And scatter glories round;

With sweetest music fill the trees,
Load with rich scent the gentle breeze,
    And strew with flowers the ground.

But when, beneath that scorching ray,
I languished, weary, through the day,
    While birds refused to sing,
Verdure decayed from field and tree,
And panting Nature mourned with me
    The freshness of the Spring.

"Wait but a little while," she said,
"Till Summer's burning days are fled;
    And Autumn shall restore,
With golden riches of her own,
And Summer's glories mellowed down,
    The freshness you deplore."

And long I waited, but in vain:
That freshness never came again,
    Though Summer passed away,
Though Autumn's mists hung cold and chill,
And drooping nature languished still,
    And sank into decay.

Till wintry blasts foreboding blew
Through leafless trees – and then I knew
    That Hope was all a dream.
But thus, fond youth, she cheated me;
And she will prove as false to thee,
    Though sweet her words may seem.'

Stern prophet! Cease thy bodings dire –
Thou canst not quench the ardent fire
    That warms the breast of youth.
Oh, let it cheer him while it may,
And gently, gently die away –
    Chilled by the damps of truth!

Tell him, that earth is not our rest;
Its joys are empty – frail at best;
    And point beyond the sky.
But gleams of light may reach us here;
And hope the *roughest* path can cheer:
    Then do not bid it fly!

Though hope may promise joys, that still
Unkindly time will ne'er fulfil;
    Or, if they come at all,
We never find them unalloyed, –
Hurtful perchance, or soon destroyed,
    They vanish or they pall;

Yet hope *itself* a brightness throws
O'er all our labours and our woes;
    While dark foreboding Care
A thousand ills will oft portend,
That Providence may ne'er intend
    The trembling heart to bear.

Or if they come, it oft appears,
Our woes are lighter than our fears,
    And far more bravely borne.
Then let us not enhance our doom;
But e'en in midnight's blackest gloom
    Expect the rising morn.

Because the road is rough and long,
Shall we despise the skylark's song,
    That cheers the wanderer's way?
Or trample down, with reckless feet,
The smiling flowerets, bright and sweet
    Because they soon decay?

Pass pleasant scenes unnoticed by,
Because the next is bleak and drear;
Or not enjoy a smiling sky,
Because a tempest may be near?

No! while we journey on our way,
We'll smile on every lovely thing;
And ever, as they pass away,
To memory and hope we'll cling.

And though that awful river flows
Before us, when the journey's past,
Perchance of all the pilgrim's woes
Most dreadful – shrink not – 'tis the last!

Though icy cold, and dark, and deep;
Beyond it smiles that blessed shore,
Where none shall suffer, none shall weep,
And bliss shall reign for evermore!

ACTON

Parting

There's no use in weeping,
Though we are condemned to part:
There's such a thing as keeping
A remembrance in one's heart:

There's such a thing as dwelling
On the thought ourselves have nurs'd,
And with scorn and courage telling
The world to do its worst.

We'll not let its follies grieve us,
We'll just take them as they come;
And then every day will leave us
A merry laugh for home.

When we've left each friend and brother,
When we're parted wide and far,
We will think of one another,
As even better than we are.

Every glorious sight above us,
Every pleasant sight beneath,
We'll connect with those that love us,
Whom we truly love till death!

In the evening, when we're sitting
By the fire perchance alone,
Then shall heart with warm heart meeting,
Give responsive tone for tone.

We can burst the bonds which chain us,
Which cold human hands have wrought,
And where none shall dare restrain us
We can meet again, in thought.

So there's no use in weeping,
Bear a cheerful spirit still;
Never doubt that Fate is keeping
Future good for present ill!

CURRER

Stanzas to —

Well, some may hate, and some may scorn,
And some may quite forget thy name;
But my sad heart must ever mourn
Thy ruined hopes, thy blighted fame!
'Twas thus I thought, an hour ago,
Even weeping o'er that wretch's woe;
One word turned back my gushing tears,
And lit my altered eye with sneers.
Then 'Bless the friendly dust,' I said,
'That hides thy unlamented head!
Vain as thou wert, and weak as vain,
The slave of Falsehood, Pride, and Pain, –
My heart has nought akin to thine;
Thy soul is powerless over mine.'

But these were thoughts that vanished too;
Unwise, unholy, and untrue:
Do I despise the timid deer,
Because his limbs are fleet with fear?
Or, would I mock the wolf's death-howl,
Because his form is gaunt and foul?
Or, hear with joy the leveret's cry,
Because it cannot bravely die?
No! Then above his memory
Let Pity's heart as tender be;
Say, 'Earth, lie lightly on that breast,
And, kind Heaven, grant that spirit rest!'

ELLIS

Appeal

Oh, I am very weary,
   Though tears no longer flow;
My eyes are tired of weeping,
   My heart is sick of woe;

My life is very lonely,
   My days pass heavily,
I'm weary of repining,
   Wilt thou not come to me?

Oh, didst thou know my longings
   For thee, from day to day,
My hopes, so often blighted,
   Thou wouldst not thus delay!

ACTON

Honour's Martyr

The moon is full this winter night;
  The stars are clear, though few;
And every window glistens bright,
  With leaves of frozen dew.

The sweet moon through your lattice gleams
  And lights your room like day;
And there you pass, in happy dreams,
  The peaceful hours away!

While I, with effort hardly quelling
  The anguish in my breast,
Wander about the silent dwelling,
  And cannot think of rest.

The old clock in the gloomy hall
  Ticks on, from hour to hour;
And every time its measured call
  Seems lingering slow and slower:

And oh, how slow that keen-eyed star
  Has tracked the chilly grey!
What, watching yet! how very far
  The morning lies away!

Without your chamber door I stand;
  Love, are you slumbering still?
My cold heart, underneath my hand,
  Has almost ceased to thrill.

Bleak, bleak the east wind sobs and sighs,
  And drowns the turret bell,
Whose sad note, undistinguished, dies
  Unheard, like my farewell!

Tomorrow, Scorn will blight my name,
  And Hate will trample me,

Will load me with a coward's shame –
 A traitor's perjury.

False friends will launch their covert sneers;
 True friends will wish me dead;
And I shall cause the bitterest tears
 That you have ever shed.

The dark deeds of my outlawed race
 Will then like virtues shine;
And men will pardon their disgrace,
 Beside the guilt of mine.

For, who forgives the accursed crime
 Of dastard treachery?
Rebellion, in its chosen time,
 May Freedom's champion be;

Revenge may stain a righteous sword,
 It may be just to slay;
But, traitor, traitor, – from *that* word
 All true breasts shrink away!

Oh, I would give my heart to death,
 To keep my honour fair;
Yet, I'll not give my inward faith
 My honour's *name* to spare!

Not even to keep your priceless love,
 Dare I, Beloved, deceive;
This treason should the future prove,
 Then, only then, believe!

I know the path I ought to go;
 I follow fearlessly,
Inquiring not what deeper woe
 Stern duty stores for me.

So foes pursue, and cold allies
 Mistrust me, every one:
Let me be false in others' eyes,
 If faithful in my own.

ELLIS

The Student's Serenade

I have slept upon my couch,
But my spirit did not rest,
For the labours of the day
Yet my weary soul opprest;

And, before my dreaming eyes
Still the learned volumes lay,
And I could not close their leaves,
And I could not turn away.

But I oped my eyes at last,
And I heard a muffled sound;
'Twas the night-breeze, come to say
That the snow was on the ground.

Then I knew that there was rest
On the mountain's bosom free;
So I left my fevered couch,
And I flew to waken thee!

I have flown to waken thee –
For, if thou wilt not arise,
Then my soul can drink no peace
From these holy moonlight skies.

And, this waste of virgin snow
To my sight will not be fair,
Unless thou wilt smiling come,
Love, to wander with me there.

Then, awake! Maria, wake!
For, if thou couldst only know
How the quiet moonlight sleeps
On this wilderness of snow,

And the groves of ancient trees,
In their snowy garb arrayed,
Till they stretch into the gloom
Of the distant valley's shade;

I know thou wouldst rejoice
To inhale this bracing air;
Thou wouldst break thy sweetest sleep
To behold a scene so fair.

O'er these wintry wilds, *alone*,
Thou wouldst joy to wander free;
And it will not please thee less,
Though that bliss be shared with me.

ACTON

Apostasy

This last denial of my faith,
    Thou, solemn Priest, hast heard;
And, though upon my bed of death,
    I call not back a word.
Point not to thy Madonna, Priest, –
    Thy sightless saint of stone;
She cannot, from this burning breast,
    Wring one repentant moan.

Thou say'st, that when a sinless child,
    I duly bent the knee,
And prayed to what in marble smiled
    Cold, lifeless, mute, on me.
I did. But listen! Children spring
    Full soon to riper youth;
And, for Love's vow and Wedlock's ring,
    I sold my early truth.

'Twas not a grey, bare head, like thine,
    Bent o'er me, when I said,
'That land and God and Faith are mine.
    For which thy fathers bled.'
I see thee not, my eyes are dim;
    But, well I hear thee say,
'O daughter, cease to think of him
    Who led thy soul astray.

Between you lies both space and time;
    Let leagues and years prevail
To turn thee from the path of crime,
    Back to the Church's pale.'
And, did I need that thou shouldst tell
    What mighty barriers rise
To part me from that dungeon-cell,
    Where my loved Walter lies?

And, did I need that thou shouldst taunt
  My dying hour at last,
By bidding this worn spirit pant
  No more for what is past?
Priest – *must* I cease to think of him?
  How hollow rings that word!
Can time, can tears, can distance dim
  The memory of my lord?

I said before, I saw not thee,
  Because, an hour agone,
Over my eye-balls, heavily,
  The lids fell down like stone.
But still my spirit's inward sight
  Beholds his image beam
As fixed, as clear, as burning bright,
  As some red planet's gleam.

Talk not of thy Last Sacrament,
  Tell not thy beads for me;
Both rite and prayer are vainly spent,
  As dews upon the sea.
Speak not one word of Heaven above,
  Rave not of Hell's alarms;
Give me but back my Walter's love,
  Restore me to his arms!

Then will the bliss of Heaven be won;
  Then will Hell shrink away,
As I have seen night's terrors shun
  The conquering steps of day.
'Tis my religion thus to love,
  My creed thus fixed to be;
Not Death shall shake, nor Priestcraft break
  My rock-like constancy!

Now go; for at the door there waits
  Another stranger guest:
He calls – I come – my pulse scarce beats,
  My heart fails in my breast.
Again that voice – how far away,
  How dreary sounds that tone!

And I, methinks, am gone astray
   In trackless wastes and lone.

I fain would rest a little while:
   Where can I find a stay,
Till dawn upon the hills shall smile,
   And show some trodden way?
'I come! I come!' in haste she said,
   ' 'Twas Walter's voice I heard!'
Then up she sprang – but fell back, dead,
   His name her latest word.

CURRER

Stanzas

I'll not weep that thou art going to leave me,
   There's nothing lovely here;
And doubly will the dark world grieve me,
   While thy heart suffers there.

I'll not weep, because the summer's glory
   Must always end in gloom;
And, follow out the happiest story –
   It closes with a tomb!

And I am weary of the anguish
   Increasing winters bear;
Weary to watch the spirit languish
   Through years of dead despair.

So, if a tear, when thou art dying,
   Should haply fall from me,
It is but that my soul is sighing,
   To go and rest with thee.

ELLIS

The Captive Dove

Poor restless dove, I pity thee;
And when I hear thy plaintive moan,
I mourn for thy captivity,
And in thy woes forget mine own.

To see thee stand prepared to fly,
And flap those useless wings of thine,
And gaze into the distant sky,
Would melt a harder heart than mine.

In vain – in vain! Thou canst not rise:
Thy prison roof confines thee there;
Its slender wires delude thine eyes,
And quench thy longings with despair.

Oh, thou wert made to wander free
In sunny mead and shady grove,
And, far beyond the rolling sea,
In distant climes, at will to rove!

Yet, hadst thou but one gentle mate
Thy little drooping heart to cheer,
And share with thee thy captive state,
Thou couldst be happy even there.

Yes, even there, if, listening by,
One faithful dear companion stood,
While gazing on her full bright eye,
Thou mightst forget thy native wood.

But thou, poor solitary dove,
Must make, unheard, thy joyless moan;
The heart, that Nature formed to love,
Must pine, neglected, and alone.

ACTON

Winter Stores

We take from life one little share,
   And say that this shall be
A space, redeemed from toil and care,
   From tears and sadness free.

And, haply, Death unstrings his bow
   And Sorrow stands apart,
And, for a little while, we know
   The sunshine of the heart.

Existence seems a summer eve,
   Warm, soft, and full of peace;
Our free, unfettered feelings give
   The soul its full release.

A moment, then, it takes the power,
   To call up thoughts that throw
Around that charmed and hallowed hour,
   This life's divinest glow.

But Time, though viewlessly it flies,
   And slowly, will not stay;
Alike, through clear and clouded skies,
   It cleaves its silent way.

Alike the bitter cup of grief,
   Alike the draught of bliss,
Its progress leaves but moment brief
   For baffled lips to kiss.

The sparkling draught is dried away,
   The hour of rest is gone,
And urgent voices, round us, say,
   'Ho, lingerer, hasten on!'

And has the soul, then, only gained,
   From this brief time of ease,
A moment's rest, when overstrained,
   One hurried glimpse of peace?

No; while the sun shone kindly o'er us,
   And flowers bloomed round our feet, –
While many a bud of joy before us
   Enclosed its petals sweet, –

An unseen work within was plying;
   Like honey-seeking bee,
From flower to flower, unwearied, flying,
   Laboured one faculty, –

Thoughtful for Winter's future sorrow,
   Its gloom and scarcity;
Prescient today, of want tomorrow,
   Toiled quiet Memory.

'Tis she that from each transient pleasure
   Extracts a lasting good;
'Tis she that finds, in summer, treasure
   To serve for winter's food.

And when Youth's summer day is vanished,
   And Age brings Winter's stress,
Her stores, with hoarded sweets replenished,
   Life's evening hours will bless.

CURRER

My Comforter

Well hast thou spoken, and yet, not taught
   A feeling strange or new;
Thou hast but roused a latent thought,
A cloud-closed beam of sunshine, brought
   To gleam in open view.

Deep down, concealed within my soul,
   That light lies hid from men;
Yet, glows unquenched – though shadows roll.
Its gentle ray cannot control,
   About the sullen den.

Was I not vexed, in these gloomy ways
   To walk alone so long?
Around me, wretches uttering praise,
Or howling o'er their hopeless days,
   And each with Frenzy's tongue; –

A brotherhood of misery,
   Their smiles as sad as sighs;
Whose madness daily maddened me,
Distorting into agony
   The bliss before my eyes!

So stood I, in Heaven's glorious sun,
   And in the glare of Hell;
My spirit drank a mingled tone,
Of seraph's songs and demon's moan;
What my soul bore, my soul alone
   Within itself may tell!

Like a soft air, above a sea,
  Tossed by the tempest's stir;
A thaw-wind, melting quietly
The snow-drift, on some wintry lea;
No: what sweet thing resembles thee,
  My thoughtful Comforter?

And yet a little longer speak,
  Calm this resentful mood;
And while the savage heart grows meek,
For other token do not seek,
But let the tear upon my cheek
  Evince my gratitude!

ELLIS

Self-Congratulation

Ellen, you were thoughtless once
  Of beauty or of grace,
Simple and homely in attire,
  Careless of form and face;
Then whence this change? and wherefore now
  So often smooth your hair?
And wherefore deck your youthful form
  With such unwearied care?

Tell us – and cease to tire our ears
  With that familiar strain –
Why will you play those simple tunes
  So often, o'er again?
'Indeed, dear friends, I can but say
  That childhood's thoughts are gone;
Each year its own new feelings brings,
  And years move swiftly on:

'And for these little simple airs –
  I love to play them o'er
So much – I dare not promise, now,
  To play them never more.'
I answered – and it was enough;
  They turned them to depart;
They could not read my secret thoughts,
  Nor see my throbbing heart.

I've noticed many a youthful form,
  Upon whose changeful face
The inmost workings of the soul
  The gazer well might trace;
The speaking eye, the changing lip,
  The ready blushing cheek,
The smiling, or beclouded brow,
  Their different feelings speak.

But, thank God! you might gaze on mine
   For hours, and never know
The secret changes of my soul
   From joy to keenest woe.
Last night, as we sat round the fire
   Conversing merrily,
We heard, without, approaching steps
   Of one well known to me!

There was no trembling in my voice,
   No blush upon my cheek,
No lustrous sparkle in my eyes,
   Of hope, or joy, to speak;
But, oh! my spirit burned within,
   My heart beat full and fast!
He came not nigh – he went away –
   And then my joy was past.

And yet my comrades marked it not:
   My voice was still the same;
They saw me smile, and o'er my face
   No signs of sadness came.
They little knew my hidden thoughts;
   And they will *never* know
The aching anguish of my heart,
   The bitter burning woe!

ACTON

The Missionary

Plough, vessel, plough the British main,
Seek the free ocean's wider plain;
Leave English scenes and English skies,
Unbind, dissever English ties;
Bear me to climes remote and strange,
Where altered life, fast-following change,
Hot action, never-ceasing toil,
Shall stir, turn, dig, the spirit's soil;
Fresh roots shall plant, fresh seed shall sow,
Till a new garden there shall grow,
Cleared of the weeds that fill it now, –
Mere human love, mere selfish yearning,
Which, cherished, would arrest me yet.
I grasp the plough, there's no returning,
Let me, then, struggle to forget.

But England's shores are yet in view,
And England's skies of tender blue
Are arched above her guardian sea.
I cannot yet Remembrance flee;
I must again, then, firmly face
That task of anguish, to retrace.
Wedded to home – I home forsake,
Fearful of change – I changes make;
Too fond of ease – I plunge in toil;
Lover of calm – I seek turmoil:
Nature and hostile Destiny
Stir in my heart a conflict wild;
And long and fierce the war will be
Ere duty both has reconciled.

What other tie yet holds me fast
To the divorced, abandoned past?
Smouldering, on my heart's altar lies
The fire of some great sacrifice,

Not yet half quenched. The sacred steel
But lately struck my carnal will,
My life-long hope, first joy and last,
What I loved well, and clung to fast;
What I wished wildly to retain,
What I renounced with soul-felt pain;
What – when I saw it, axe-struck, perish –
Left me no joy on earth to cherish;
A man bereft – yet sternly now
I do confirm that Jephtha vow:
Shall I retract, or fear, or flee?
Did Christ, when rose the fatal tree
Before him, on Mount Calvary?
'Twas a long fight, hard fought, but won,
And what I did was justly done.

Yet, Helen! from thy love I turned,
When my heart most for thy heart burned;
I dared thy tears, I dared thy scorn –
Easier the death-pang had been borne.
Helen! thou mightst not go with me,
I could not – dared not stay for thee!
I heard, afar, in bonds complain
The savage from beyond the main;
And that wild sound rose o'er the cry
Wrung out by passion's agony;
And even when, with the bitterest tear
I ever shed, mine eyes were dim,
Still, with the spirit's vision clear,
I saw Hell's empire, vast and grim,
Spread on each Indian river's shore,
Each realm of Asia covering o'er.

There, the weak, trampled by the strong,
Live but to suffer – hopeless die;
There pagan-priests, whose creed is Wrong,
Extortion, Lust, and Cruelty,
Crush our lost race – and brimming fill
The bitter cup of human ill;
And I – who have the healing creed,

The faith benign of Mary's Son;
Shall I behold my brother's need
And, selfishly, to aid him shun?
I – who upon my mother's knees,
In childhood, read Christ's written word,
Received his legacy of peace,
His holy rule of action heard;
I – in whose heart the sacred sense
Of Jesus' love was early felt;
Of his pure full benevolence,
His pitying tenderness for guilt;
His shepherd-care for wandering sheep,
For all weak, sorrowing, trembling things,
His mercy vast, his passion deep
Of anguish for man's sufferings;
I – schooled from childhood in such lore –
Dared I draw back or hesitate,
When called to heal the sickness sore
Of those far off and desolate?
Dark, in the realm and shades of Death.
Nations and tribes and empires lie,
But even to them the light of Faith
Is breaking on their sombre sky:
And be it mine to bid them raise
Their drooped heads to the kindling scene,
And know and hail the sunrise blaze
Which heralds Christ the Nazarene.
I know how Hell the veil will spread
Over their brows and filmy eyes,
And earthward crush the lifted head
That would look up and seek the skies;
I know what war the fiend will wage
Against that soldier of the cross,
Who comes to dare his demon rage,
And work his kingdom shame and loss.
Yes, hard and terrible the toil
Of him who steps on foreign soil,
Resolved to plant the gospel vine,
Where tyrants rule and slaves repine;
Eager to lift Religion's light

Where thickest shades of mental night
Screen the false god and fiendish rite;
Reckless that missionary blood,
Shed in wild wilderness and wood,
Has left, upon the unblest air,
The man's deep moan – the martyr's prayer.
I know my lot – I only ask
Power to fulfil the glorious task;
Willing the spirit, may the flesh
Strength for the day receive afresh.
May burning sun or deadly wind
Prevail not o'er an earnest mind;
May torments strange or direst death
Nor trample truth, nor baffle faith.
Though such blood-drops should fall from me
As fell in old Gethsemane,
Welcome the anguish, so it gave
More strength to work – more skill to save.
And, oh! if brief must be my time,
If hostile hand or fatal clime
Cut short my course – still o'er my grave,
Lord, may thy harvest whitening wave.
So I the culture may begin,
Let others thrust the sickle in;
If but the seed will faster grow,
May my blood water what I sow!

What! have I ever trembling stood,
And feared to give to God that blood?
What! has the coward love of life
Made me shrink from the righteous strife?
Have human passions, human fears
Severed me from those Pioneers,
Whose task is to march first, and trace
Paths for the progress of our race?
It has been so; but grant me, Lord,
Now to stand steadfast by thy word!
Protected by salvation's helm,
Shielded by faith – with truth begirt,
To smile when trials seek to whelm

And stand 'mid testing fires unhurt!
Hurling hell's strongest bulwarks down,
Even when the last pang thrills my breast,
When Death bestows the Martyr's crown,
And calls me into Jesus' rest.
Then for my ultimate reward –
Then for the world-rejoicing word –
The voice from Father – Spirit – Son:
'Servant of God, well hast thou done!'

                                        CURRER

The Old Stoic

Riches I hold in light esteem;
  And Love I laugh to scorn;
And lust of fame was but a dream
  That vanished with the morn:

And if I pray, the only prayer
  That moves my lips for me
Is, 'Leave the heart that now I bear,
  And give me liberty!'

Yes, as my swift days near their goal,
  'Tis all that I implore;
In life and death, a chainless soul,
  With courage to endure.

ELLIS

Fluctuations

What though the Sun had left my sky;
  To save me from despair
The blessed Moon arose on high,
  And shone serenely there.

I watched her, with a tearful gaze,
  Rise slowly o'er the hill,
While through the dim horizon's haze
  Her light gleamed faint and chill.

I thought such wan and lifeless beams
　　Could ne'er my heart repay,
For the bright sun's most transient gleams
　　That cheered me through the day:

But as above that mist's control
　　She rose, and brighter shone,
I felt her light upon my soul;
　　But now – that light is gone!

Thick vapours snatched her from my sight,
　　And I was darkling left,
All in the cold and gloomy night,
　　Of light and hope bereft:

Until, methought, a little star
　　Shone forth with trembling ray,
To cheer me with its light afar –
　　But that, too, passed away.

Anon, an earthly meteor blazed
　　The gloomy darkness through;
I smiled, yet trembled while I gazed –
　　But that soon vanished too!

And darker, drearier fell the night
　　Upon my spirit then; –
But what is that faint struggling light?
　　Is it the Moon again?

Kind Heaven! increase that silvery gleam,
　　And bid these clouds depart,
And let her soft celestial beam
　　Restore my fainting heart!

ACTON

INDEX OF POEM TITLES

INDEX OF FIRST LINES

Not in scorn do I reprove thee 101

'O Day! he cannot die 36
O God! if this indeed be all 69
Oh, I am very weary 121
Oh, thy bright eyes must answer now 103
Oh, weep not, love! each tear that springs 52
On a sunny brae, alone I lay 77

Plough, vessel, plough the British main 136
Poor restless dove, I pity thee 129

Riches I hold in light esteem 141

She will not sleep, for fear of dreams 42
'Sister, you've sat there all the day 87
Sit still – a word – a breath may break 25
Some have won a wild delight 99
Sweet are thy strains, celestial Bard 80

'The evening passes fast away 107
The human heart has hidden treasures 106
The linnet in the rocky dells 38
The moon is full this winter night 122
The room is quiet, thoughts alone 94
'The winter wind is loud and wild 8
There should be no despair for you 97
There's no use in weeping 118
This last denial of my faith 126
Though bleak these woods, and damp the ground 104
'Tis strange to think, there *was* a time 98

Warm is the parlour atmosphere 57
We take from life one little share 130
Well hast thou spoken, and yet, not taught 132
Well, some may hate, and some may scorn 120
What is she writing? Watch her now 74
What though the Sun had left my sky 141
When sinks my heart in hopeless gloom 113
When weary with the long day's care 83

Yes, thou art gone! and never more 10
You may rejoice to think *yourselves* secure 92